THE SiLVER BOY

Also by Kristina Ohlsson

The Glass Children

For adult readers:

Unwanted

Silenced

The Disappeared

Hostage

Stars of David

Kristina Ohlsson

THE SiLVER BOY

Translated by Marlaine Delargy

CORGI YEARLING

CORGI YEARLING

UK | USA | Canada | Ireland | Australia
India | New Zealand | South Africa

Corgi Yearling is part of the Penguin Random House group of companies whose
addresses can be found at global.penguinrandomhouse.com.

www.penguin.co.uk
www.puffinbooks.co.uk
www.ladybird.co.uk

Penguin
Random House
UK

Swedish edition published 2014 (as *Silverpojken* by Lilla Piratförlaget)
This edition published 2017

001

Set in ITC New Baskerville

Typeset in India by Thomson Digital Pvt Ltd, Noida, Delhi

Printed in Great Britain by Clays Ltd, St Ives plc

A CIP catalogue record for this book is available from the British Library.

ISBN: 978-0-440-87117-0

MIX
Paper from
responsible sources
FSC® C018179

Penguin Random House is committed to a
sustainable future for our business, our readers
and our planet. This book is made from Forest
Stewardship Council® certified paper

Chapter One

The first time Aladdin saw the boy in the short trousers it was snowing. The sky was heavy with thick clouds, and it was cold. Aladdin was going ice-skating with his friend Billie; the river that ran through the middle of Åhus had frozen, turning the narrow strip of water into a shining ice rink. Aladdin's father said he couldn't remember the last time that had happened.

'I've lived in Åhus for almost ten years, and I've never seen the river freeze as early as November,' he said.

Aladdin listened as he tucked a sandwich and a flask of hot chocolate into his rucksack.

His mother and father had moved to Sweden from Turkey when Aladdin was a little boy. He couldn't remember anything about it. If anyone asked where he came from, he always said 'Åhus'.

On the day he saw the boy in the short trousers, he was in a hurry. He knew he was late, and he didn't want Billie to have to wait for him.

Then again, these days it wasn't actually Aladdin's fault that he was late. It was all down to his parents; they had decided to sell their house and move into the old water tower where their restaurant, the Turk in the Tower, was situated.

'What do you mean, we're going to live in the water tower?' Aladdin had said. 'Are you crazy? We can't do that!'

'Why not?' his mother had replied. 'We own the whole building, but we only use the top floor and the bottom floor for the restaurant. The rest of the place is empty.'

And that was exactly what had happened; just a few weeks ago they had moved in, and now Aladdin had to run up five flights of stairs to get to his room, which was why he was often late meeting his friends. His mother joked and said it was good for him, and that he would develop strong legs. Aladdin didn't find her comments remotely amusing. After all, he knew the real reason behind the move.

The restaurant wasn't doing too well. They weren't earning as much money any more, so first of all they had sold the house, then the houseboat on which they used to live in the summer.

'It's the same for everyone; sometimes you have more money, sometimes you have less,' Aladdin's father said. 'It's nothing to worry about.'

But Aladdin could see that he was anxious, and it didn't feel right. Not one little bit.

'Just be careful,' Aladdin's mother said when he had finished packing his rucksack. 'Just remember that the river is only frozen right up at the top end, not further down where the boats are.'

'Yeah yeah,' Aladdin said as he dashed off.

His mother called him back. 'Don't be late for dinner. Your dad and I want to talk to you.' She looked serious.

Aladdin frowned. 'Has something happened?'

'We'll talk about it later. Off you go – have fun with Billie!'

With that she turned away and went back to the restaurant. Aladdin made his way slowly down the stairs. What did his parents want to talk to him about?

Just as he walked out through the front door, he saw the boy. He was standing a short distance away looking at Aladdin, who was so surprised he almost dropped the rucksack he was clutching in his arms.

'Hi,' he said automatically.

The boy was standing next to the restaurant sign that Aladdin's father had put up. There was something peculiar about him. In spite of the cold weather, he was wearing only short trousers and a black and white striped jumper. The trousers were made of some kind of thick green material; Aladdin thought they looked scratchy. Below them were long socks and boots. Black leather boots, scuffed and worn.

The boy didn't respond to Aladdin's greeting; he just stood there in the snow, staring. Aladdin hesitated. Perhaps he ought to stop – maybe the boy needed help?

'Are you lost?' Aladdin asked.

He felt stupid. *Lost?* The boy looked about twelve years old, the same age as Aladdin. If he was lost, he wouldn't be standing there in the snow staring at Aladdin.

Still the boy didn't speak. He looked away and set off towards the tower. Were his parents in the restaurant?

But the boy didn't go inside; he disappeared round the side of the tower. Aladdin glanced at his watch; he really didn't have time for this. He was already late. But his curiosity got the better of him – he just had to see where the boy had gone.

Quickly he swung the rucksack onto his back and hurried round the tower. But after just a few metres he stopped dead. There was no sign of the boy.

'Hello?' Aladdin called.

No reply.

Weird.

He gazed all around, unsure what to do next. It was as if the ground had opened up and simply swallowed the boy.

Chapter Two

'What do you mean, he disappeared?' Billie said.

She and Aladdin were sitting on the jetty by the river, putting on their skates.

'He just disappeared,' Aladdin said again. 'He went round the side of the tower, and then – pouf! Nothing. He just wasn't there any more.'

Aladdin had run all the way to the river, and had only been a couple of minutes late.

'That sounds weird,' Billie said. 'Surely he must have been frozen if he was in short trousers?'

'I don't know. He didn't look cold. And he was wearing long socks.'

'Long socks,' Billie giggled.

She tied one last knot in the laces of her skates and stood up. There were already lots of people on the ice. She bent down and took something out of a carrier bag she had brought with her.

A lifejacket.

Aladdin burst out laughing. 'You're not going to wear that, are you?'

'I have to,' Billie said. 'Otherwise Mum will go mad. She said I wasn't allowed on the ice without a lifejacket.'

Billie was the size of a small elephant by the time she had put it on over her thick winter jacket. She pulled on her helmet, squashing her woolly hat down over her forehead.

She sighed as Aladdin carried on laughing.

'OK, let's go,' he said, setting off on wobbly legs.

'Mum said we have to stick to the parts where we're sure the ice is thick enough,' Billie said.

'My mum said exactly the same thing.'

'And we're not allowed to go anywhere near the refugee boat either.'

The refugee boat was a large fishing boat moored in the harbour. It had simply appeared one morning, packed with people from another country. The newspapers had started calling it the refugee boat. Nobody seemed to know what was going to happen to the boat itself, or to the people on board. Aladdin didn't even know where they were from, but he did know why they wouldn't leave the boat; it was because they wanted to stay in Sweden, and they didn't want to end up in some refugee reception centre. If they were forced to leave Åhus, perhaps they would just sail away one night.

The harbour was long and narrow; it didn't widen out until it reached the sea. In spite of the fact that it was early winter, Aladdin was already longing for the summer, when the ice-cream boat would open up and there would be lots of people in the village. Åhus was so gloomy and quiet in the winter.

Neither Billie nor Aladdin were particularly good at ice-skating, but it was still fun. They had just passed one of the restaurants by the harbour when two older boys came whizzing along, moving far too fast. Aladdin didn't have time to work out what was happening; he just felt someone cannon into him, and he lost his balance. The ice was cold and hard as he landed on his stomach.

'Look where you're going!' Billie shouted crossly, but the two boys just laughed and kept on going.

'Idiots,' Aladdin muttered as he struggled to his feet. His knees twinged as he straightened up.

'Did you hurt yourself?' Billie asked anxiously.

'I'm fine,' Aladdin said, brushing the snow off his clothes.

And that was when he saw the boy in the green short trousers again. On a small hill behind the restaurants lay the remains of an old castle. The boy was standing on the castle wall, gazing out across the ice.

'There!' Aladdin said, pointing. 'Can you see him? Up on the wall?'

Billie looked. 'I can't see anybody.'

'Are you blind?' Aladdin said crossly, looking over at her. 'He's there, on the castle wall!'

He pointed again, his breath turning to mist in the cold air.

Slowly he lowered his arm.

The boy had disappeared. Again.

Chapter Three

There was a wonderful aroma of garlic. Aladdin's mum and dad had brought chicken and rice down from the restaurant for dinner. He had been so busy thinking about the boy who had disappeared that he had forgotten they wanted to talk to him about something. But now he remembered.

There was silence around the table. A peculiar kind of silence. And it was odd that all three of them were eating together; that hadn't happened for a long time. Mum and Dad were nearly always working.

Eventually his mum spoke up. 'Aladdin, we're sorry to have to ask you this, but . . . have you taken any food from the restaurant?'

Aladdin was so surprised that he hardly knew what to say. 'No. Why would I do that?'

He knew that he wasn't allowed to take anything from the restaurant without asking first. Which he always did.

'The thing is,' his father said, looking slightly relieved, 'food has been going missing from the kitchen.'

'How much food?' Aladdin asked.

'Quite a lot, actually,' his mother replied. 'At first we didn't pay much attention, but today all the Mirja meatballs had gone, which was a nuisance because customers had to sit and wait while I made a fresh batch.'

Aladdin's Turkish grandmother had given his parents her recipe for meatballs, so they were named after her. They were very popular with customers, so his father usually kept a good stock in the freezer.

'That's weird,' Aladdin said.

He still didn't quite know what to say; did his own parents really think he'd turned into a thief? If so, it was a bit upsetting.

'What makes you think it was me?' he said. 'I mean, it could be anybody!'

His parents both started talking at the same time.

'It's just that it's been going on for over a week now,' his mother explained. 'There's food in the freezer at night, and the following morning it's gone. There aren't many people who have access to the kitchen overnight.'

That was true, of course. Only Aladdin and his parents could get into the restaurant when it was closed. But then he thought of something.

'Mats has a set of keys.'

Mats was his parents' right-hand man in the restaurant. He did the shopping, the cleaning and the washing-up, and he was also responsible for minor repairs.

'That occurred to us as well,' his father said. 'But Mats is loyal, you know that. He would never do such a thing.'

Aladdin didn't believe they could be sure of that. 'Maybe he lent the key to someone else? Someone who came in and stole food without Mats knowing anything about it?'

His parents looked worried.

12

'You could be right,' his father said. 'But in that case I'd like to know what he's doing lending our key to a stranger.'

Aladdin's mother looked at him with tenderness in her eyes. 'I was hoping it was you who'd taken the food, sweetheart. I thought maybe one of your friends had problems at home and you were trying to help, but I guess that's not the case.'

Aladdin didn't say anything for a little while. He still thought his parents were hiding something from him; something bigger than the mystery of the missing food.

'Has anything else happened?' he said eventually.

His parents looked at one another, then at Aladdin.

'Well,' his father began. 'Maybe. It's not something we need to go into in detail right now, but . . . you know we've had problems recently? Financial problems, I mean.'

Aladdin nodded. 'That's why we sold the house and the boat.'

'Exactly,' his mother said. 'It's just that things haven't really improved. They've got worse, in fact.'

'Worse?'

'As I said, we don't need to go into detail right now,' his father said quickly.

'But . . .'

Aladdin's mother shook her head. 'It's nothing for you to worry about, Aladdin. Think about the food and tell us if you come up with any ideas about who might have taken it. If we didn't have these other problems, we could have laughed it off, but right now it's a serious matter.'

Aladdin was about to say they were wrong, that it concerned the whole family if they were running out of money. But then it occurred to him that perhaps there was someone else who could be stealing food.

'I saw a boy today when I went skating. He was wearing short trousers even though it was freezing cold. He was standing in the snow when I left here; I wonder if he could have taken the food . . .'

'A boy? In short trousers?' his father repeated slowly.

Aladdin nodded. 'I saw him twice, once in the garden and then down by the river. He was standing on the castle wall.'

His mother patted her hair to make sure the thick braid was intact. 'Perhaps he's one of the children from the refugee boat,' she said. 'Those poor souls are still living on board.'

Aladdin's father looked almost relieved. 'Come and tell us next time you see him so that we can have a word with him. He's welcome to all the food I can spare, but it would be easier if he didn't steal from us. If it is him, of course.'

'But how would he get in?' his mother said. 'The doors are locked all night.'

'Perhaps he comes in while the restaurant is open, then hides away until we've gone to bed? There are plenty of hiding places in the tower.'

His mother shuddered. 'I can cope with the thought of a child running around in here, but that's something we ought to think about – anyone could wait inside the tower after we've closed.'

Aladdin felt a chill run down his spine. Someone was getting in at night and stealing food. Could it really be the boy in short trousers? He decided it didn't really matter who it was.

Someone was coming into their tower, their home, without asking permission.

Someone was taking stuff from their restaurant.

That wasn't just wrong. It was horrible.

Chapter Four

It was the weekend again, and Aladdin and Billie were sitting in Aladdin's room eating sweets. It was snowing, and neither of them wanted to go out. More food had gone missing from the restaurant. Aladdin hadn't seen any sign of the boy in the short trousers, and was starting to wonder if he had imagined the whole thing.

'A thief?' Billie said. 'For real?'

They hadn't seen each other all week. Aladdin had been busy with school, homework, piano lessons and his model planes. He didn't know what Billie had been up to, but she'd probably had homework too. And she'd probably read a load of books; Aladdin didn't know anyone who read as much as Billie.

'For real,' he said. 'Someone is sneaking into our tower at night and stealing food. My parents think it might be one of the refugee kids from the boat.'

'Haven't they called the police?'

Aladdin sighed. Of course they had, but apparently the police had more important things to do than search for stolen meatballs.

'Perhaps I could have a word with Josef,' Billie suggested. 'I'm sure he could help.'

Josef was a police officer, and a friend of Billie's mother.

'That would be brilliant,' Aladdin said; he liked Josef. 'But don't mention that the thief could be a child; Dad doesn't want the police involved if that is the case.'

Deep down, Aladdin wondered what Josef could do. For almost a week his father had stayed up each night keeping watch on the stairs – only for a few hours, to be fair, because he had to get some sleep – but he had seen nothing. And still food was disappearing from the fridge; the latest thing was a big batch of fruit salad that his mother had made during the evening.

Billie took another sweet. 'Does it really matter if a little bit of food goes missing?' she said. 'I mean, your parents have loads of food. And loads of money.'

Aladdin stared at the floor. He knew that lots of people shared Billie's opinion; they thought his parents must be rich, just because they owned a restaurant.

'I don't think we've got much money left,' he said quietly. 'That's why they're so worried about this food. What if the thief starts taking other stuff?'

His father had talked about money quite a lot lately, usually when he thought Aladdin wasn't listening. Aladdin didn't know much about financial matters, but he realized that everything cost money. If you couldn't pay for what you needed, you had problems. Big problems, if you were unlucky.

Billie's face grew serious as she listened to his explanation. 'We have to do something,' she said firmly. 'Couldn't it be that guy who's always so miserable? The guy who works in the restaurant? What's his name . . . Mats! That's it, Mats. It seems as if the thief gets in using a key, doesn't it?'

'We thought of that, but Dad has spoken to Mats and it's not him. Apparently.'

Aladdin wasn't completely convinced. He had never liked Mats; not because he was stupid or unpleasant, but because he was weird. His parents liked him because he was good at his job; he was quick and efficient. But Aladdin wondered why he was always so miserable. And he was huge. If you were in the kitchen while Mats was washing up, it was impossible to ignore him.

Billie didn't like Mats either. 'What do you mean, your dad's spoken to him? If Mats is the thief, he's hardly going to admit it, is he? You have to catch him red-handed!'

Aladdin smiled. *Catch him red-handed* – that was exactly how he and Billie had caught a ghost not long after Billie had moved to Åhus.

'Dad didn't just speak to him,' he explained. 'Apparently Mats was away on several occasions when food went missing, so it can't be him.'

Aladdin had known Billie for just a few months. They had become friends during the summer when she and her mum moved to Åhus from Kristianstad. Aladdin knew that Billie had hated living here at first, so she still went to her old school in Kristianstad, even though it was over ten miles away. Aladdin wished she would change her mind and transfer to the school in Åhus, because then they would be in the same class.

'We ought to spy on Mats, then we'd know for sure,' Billie said. 'He might be lying. Maybe he wasn't away at all!'

Aladdin burst out laughing. 'You're joking! We can't do that! You can't just go around spying on people!'

'Of course you can! And it's important. What if your parents run out of money – what will you do then?'

That was something Aladdin really didn't want to think about. They *couldn't* run out of money. They just couldn't.

'Is Mats working today?' Billie asked.

Aladdin shook his head. It was Saturday, and Mats had a day off. 'He said he was going to Malmö to visit his mother. He won't be back until tomorrow.'

'Typical,' Billie said. Then her face lit up. 'Actually, that's perfect!'

'What are you talking about?'

'Well, he said he was going away, so we can go round to his place and see if he's there. Then we'll know if he's lying.'

Aladdin wasn't so sure. 'How's that going to work? He knows both of us – what are we supposed to say if we bump into him?'

Billie thought for a moment. 'We'll call Simona and get her to come over on the bus. He doesn't know her.'

Simona lived in Kristianstad; she was Billie's friend, and had become friends with Aladdin too.

He thought about it, and decided it was a good idea. 'OK. I'll go and find Mats's address.'

Easier said than done. Mats had such a common name that it was impossible to look up the address on the internet; there were far too many matches. Aladdin definitely didn't want to ask his parents, so he sneaked into their bedroom to look for his mother's handbag. She always carried her address book, and Mats was bound to be in there. He looked everywhere, but he couldn't find the handbag.

He ran down to the office; it was a mess as usual, with files and papers all over the place.

Sighing to himself, Aladdin switched on the light and started searching through the chaos on the desk. Perhaps there was something that was due to be sent to Mats – his payslip, maybe?

Aladdin didn't want anyone to know he had been there, but it was hard not to leave any signs; it was impossible to remember exactly how everything had looked when he started. He was just about to give up when he spotted an envelope with Mats's name on it. It was sealed, so he didn't know what was inside, but that didn't matter. The important thing was the address.

He recognized his mother's handwriting:

Mats Eriksson
Getingvägen 41
Åhus

Getingvägen. That wasn't far from Billie's house. Perfect. Aladdin ran back up to his room. Billie was in the bathroom; it sounded as if she was washing her hands. Aladdin found a piece of paper and wrote down the address. He glanced out of the window and noticed that it had stopped snowing. Good – that would make things much easier.

But then he saw something that made him forget both Mats and the missing food.

The boy in the short trousers was standing in the snow at the bottom of the tower, right next to the restaurant sign. Exactly where Aladdin had seen him the first time.

Aladdin didn't move.

The boy in the snow didn't move either.

Billie emerged from the bathroom. 'What are you looking at?'

Aladdin didn't take his eyes off the boy. He wasn't wearing the same clothes this time; he had a jacket on instead of a jumper.

'The boy in the short trousers,' he whispered in answer to Billie's question, as if he was afraid that the boy would hear him if he spoke any louder.

Billie moved closer and looked out. 'Where?'

'Can't you see him?' Aladdin said impatiently. 'There!'

The boy started walking, and disappeared from view. He seemed to be heading round the back of the tower.

Aladdin dashed out of his room and down the stairs.

'Where are you going?' Billie called after him.

He didn't even think about what he was doing, he simply ran. Straight out of the door and into the snow. In his socks. He was panting as he raced round the tower.

Not again, he thought as he stopped to catch his breath.

The boy had disappeared once more.

Aladdin was all alone, his heart pounding. For the first time he was really scared. How come the boy was always so quick? Why didn't he stay around and say what he wanted?

Chapter Five

Aladdin's feet had almost turned to ice by the time he got back into the warmth. His mother was waiting for him; she had seen him go running out into the snow in his socks.

'Have you lost your mind?' she shouted in Turkish. 'Going outside with no shoes on! You'll catch your death of cold!'

Then she caught sight of Billie and softened. She and Aladdin's father always spoke Turkish to their son, but not when he had friends round.

'Your father and I have a job to do,' she said. 'On Saturdays too. You're too old to do something this stupid, Aladdin.'

He pulled off his socks. 'I saw him again,' he said. 'The boy in the short trousers.'

His mother looked confused; then she remembered what he was talking about. 'The refugee boy,' she said. 'Did you speak to him?'

'No. He . . . disappeared.'

'Disappeared?'

'I suppose he was too fast for me,' Aladdin muttered.

His mother looked at Billie. 'Did you see this boy too?'

Billie wasn't quite sure what to say. 'No. Yes. Maybe. But he was really fast, like Aladdin said.'

Aladdin's mother gazed at him for a long time.

'I'm not lying,' he insisted. He felt stupid, standing there with a wet sock in each hand.

'I'm sure you're not. I'm going to search the whole tower right now; perhaps he's hiding somewhere.'

But however hard Aladdin's mother looked, there was no sign of the boy anywhere in the tower.

'Are you absolutely sure you saw him?' Billie whispered.

'Of course I am!' Aladdin hissed.

His mother slowly shook her head when she had finished searching. 'Strange,' she said. 'Very strange.'

Simona was due to arrive on the bus an hour later; Billie and Aladdin went down to meet her. As Billie had expected, Simona was happy to spy on Mats's house. Aladdin liked Simona; she was cool. Much cooler than him. And braver. And she always said exactly what she thought.

Neither Billie nor Aladdin had much to say on their way to the bus stop. Aladdin kept kicking at the snow; it bothered him that Billie hadn't seen the boy.

'Maybe he's a ghost,' he muttered.

Billie laughed. 'But you don't believe in ghosts!'

'Neither do you!'

Billie fell silent, and Aladdin knew why. For a while they had thought that Billie's house was haunted. It felt like such a long time ago now, although in fact it was only a few months. To be honest, they still weren't completely sure whether the house was haunted or not. They had managed to find the explanation for most of the spooky things that had happened, but not all of them. The ceiling light in the living room still swung slowly to and fro from time to time – in spite of the fact that all the doors and windows were closed.

'There could be a draught from the air vents,' Billie's mother said firmly when they tried to talk to her about it.

Billie had told Aladdin that it didn't bother her; the light could swing to and fro as much as it wanted, as long as things didn't go back to the way they had been at the start, with someone tapping on the windows in the middle of the night and leaving messages in the spare room.

Aladdin thought about the boy in the strange clothes. Of course he wasn't a ghost. There was no such thing as ghosts. And yet he frightened Aladdin. Every single time.

What does he want? Aladdin wondered.

They had to run the last few metres to the bus stop; Simona met them with a big smile.

'I'm so glad you called!' she said to Billie. 'I couldn't wait to get out of the house; my mum and dad are just arguing all the time.'

Aladdin had heard her say the same thing several times. His own parents hardly ever argued – at least, that was the way it had been, but something had changed. Since he first heard his father say they were having financial problems, there had been quite a few rows.

'Can we go past the harbour and check out the refugee boat?' Simona asked. 'It's been in the paper.'

'There's not much to see,' Aladdin said doubtfully. 'It's just an old boat.'

In his class, only Aladdin and two others had parents who came from countries other than Sweden, but he hardly ever thought about it. Why should it matter where a person was from? His father always said how pleased he was that they had come to Sweden ten years ago, because if they had arrived today, everything would have been much more difficult. When he said that, Aladdin wondered what it would have been like if they had stayed in Turkey, but he just couldn't imagine it. He felt every bit as Swedish as Simona and Billie and everyone else. Nor could he imagine what life was like on the refugee boat. Aladdin and his parents had come to Sweden by plane; the very thought of hiding in a freezing cold fishing boat for weeks on end made him feel ill.

'So what are we doing?' Simona asked as they set off from the bus stop. 'Spying on some old guy?'

Aladdin wouldn't exactly call Mats an old guy; he was about the same age as Aladdin's father, and *he* definitely wasn't old. But he couldn't argue about the spying . . .

Billie explained to Simona what had been going on.

'Wow,' Simona said. 'A thief. But why would this Mats need to steal food? Is he hungry?'

'We don't really know,' Aladdin said.

The whole thing was just stupid. Why should they assume that Mats was the thief when they didn't know why he was taking the food? But if it wasn't Mats, then who could it be?

'Perhaps he's got a big family that nobody knows about,' Billie suggested.

'Yeah, right,' Aladdin said.

'Why not?'

Simona interrupted them. 'Is it far?'

'We're almost there,' Aladdin reassured her. 'He lives near Billie.'

A few minutes later they were standing a short distance away from Mats's house.

'It's that one,' Aladdin said, pointing across the road. It was almost three o'clock; soon the sun would disappear. Aladdin shuddered; he wanted to get home before dark.

The house lay silent and gloomy. The wind whispered in the tall pine trees along the road.

'It looks empty,' Billie said.

'We can't be sure unless we ring the doorbell,' Aladdin said, turning to Simona. 'Or, to put it more accurately, unless *you* ring the doorbell. Are you ready?'

Sometimes a plan seemed like such a brilliant idea when you came up with it. And then it didn't seem like a very good idea at all when you actually had to carry it out. Simona wasn't scared, but as she was about to set off across the road, she hesitated.

'Can you just run the whole thing by me one more time?'

'Someone has been stealing food from Aladdin's parents,' Billie began. 'We think it could be Mats, but Aladdin's father has spoken to him, and says it's not him. Mats claims he's been away on several occasions when food has gone missing, but who knows if that's true?'

Aladdin took over: 'It's his day off today, and he said he was going to Malmö to visit his mother. So we thought we'd check to see if he really does go away as often as he says, or if he's lying.'

'And that's why you want me to ring the door-bell? To see if he's home?'

'Exactly,' Aladdin said. 'He knows me and Billie, but he won't recognize you.'

Simona thought for a moment, then she came up with the same question as Billie had asked:

'Why does it matter if the odd bit of food is going missing from your restaurant?'

Aladdin felt uncomfortable; he didn't know Simona as well as he knew Billie.

'Aladdin's parents are kind of short of money at the moment,' Billie said before he could stop her. 'And we're afraid the thief will start taking other stuff instead of food. Valuable stuff.'

'OK,' said Simona, straightening up. 'Now I get it. What do I say if he opens the door?'

'Anything you like,' Billie said. 'Tell him you'll be selling Christmas magazines in a few weeks; ask him if he's interested in buying one and say you'll call back if he is.'

'Although obviously you don't need to do that,' Aladdin quickly chipped in. 'Call back, I mean.'

'Obviously,' Simona said.

A car drove past and made them jump.

'Hurry up,' Billie said. 'Then we can go back to mine for a drink.'

Simona set off, then turned round. 'You are staying here to keep an eye on the house, aren't you?'

'Of course,' Aladdin said.

He didn't really believe that Mats was dangerous, but you could never be sure.

Aladdin and Billie moved behind some tall bushes so that they could see the house without being seen. Aladdin shuffled his feet nervously as he watched Simona walk up the drive. She went up the steps and rang the doorbell. Several times. No one came.

She went back down the steps, but she didn't leave as Aladdin had expected. Instead she turned right and headed off round the corner of the house.

'What's she doing?' Billie hissed. 'We can't see her any more!'

Aladdin swallowed; he had a pain in his stomach. This didn't feel good.

Another car came along the road, but this time Aladdin and Billie were ready; as it drove past, they moved a little further behind the bushes. Aladdin craned his neck to watch the car; it began to brake, as if it was about to stop.

There was still no sign of Simona.

'I wish she'd hurry up,' Billie muttered.

She fell silent as she saw the car turn into Mats's drive. Only then did Aladdin see who was behind the wheel.

It was Mats.

Chapter Six

The car door slammed and Mats marched towards the house, his tall figure casting a long shadow across the white snow.

Then he stopped, as if he had suddenly turned to ice. It looked as if he had spotted something that bothered him.

'Oh no,' Billie whispered. 'Simona's footprints in the snow.'

Aladdin was so nervous that he almost forgot to breathe.

Slowly Mats moved towards the steps. He stopped again, staring at the trail of footprints leading round the side of the house.

A thousand thoughts were spinning around in

Aladdin's head. What should they do? What if Mats was dangerous after all?

Billie nudged him. 'What are we going to do?' she whispered.

'I don't know,' Aladdin said in despair.

To their great relief, Mats decided not to follow the footprints, and went into the house instead. He had only just shut the door behind him when Simona came racing round the corner. She must have heard the car, and waited for Mats to go inside. She shot across the snow like an arrow, heading for the road; she had almost made it when Mats opened the door.

'Stop!' he shouted. 'Stop right there! This is private property – what do you think you're doing?'

But Simona didn't stop. She ran down the road as fast as she could, past the bushes where Billie and Aladdin were hiding and on towards Billie's house. Mats stood there watching her for a moment, then he went back indoors.

At which point Billie and Aladdin took to their heels as well.

*

Simona was waiting on Billie's patio.

'I thought you'd never get here,' she said when she saw them. Billie and Aladdin were both gasping for breath. Billie dug out her key.

'We had to wait until he'd gone back in,' Aladdin said.

'At least you know he's lying now,' Simona said. 'He certainly wasn't away.'

'We need to tell your parents,' Billie said to Aladdin.

'It can wait until tomorrow. Let's see if any food goes missing tonight – otherwise I don't think Mum and Dad will be all that bothered about why Mats was lying.'

They took off their outdoor clothes and hung them up in the hallway. The house was lovely and warm. No one was home, but there was a note on the kitchen table:

Billie – Josef and I have gone for a walk.
We'll be home in an hour or so.
Love Mum
xx

37

'Is Josef here often?' Simon asked.

Billie shrugged. 'Sometimes. Pretty often, I suppose.'

'Is he going to move in?'

'I don't know,' Billie said. 'I don't think that's what Mum wants. Not yet.'

Billie's father had died just over a year ago. Aladdin had never said anything to Billie, but he couldn't think of anything worse than his mum being with someone other than his dad. Not even if his dad died.

'Josef's cool,' he said, mainly for the sake of something to say.

He really did think Josef was cool. And he was a police officer, which also made him cool in Aladdin's eyes.

Billie went and fetched some juice from the kitchen. It was her grandmother who made the juice for her. Aladdin's grandmother never made juice. Just meatballs.

'What are you going to do tonight?' Simona asked.

Billie and Aladdin looked at one another.

'Tonight?' Billie said.

'Well, yes – you've got to try and expose Mats once and for all,' Simona said, looking at Aladdin. 'Catch him stealing so that you can prove to your mum and dad that he's the thief.'

Aladdin hadn't thought that far ahead. 'I think it's enough that we know he was lying,' he said. 'Let's see if any food goes missing tonight before we do anything else.'

Simona frowned. 'Wouldn't it be better to stay up all night to see what happens?' she said.

Billie looked doubtful. 'I don't think I could stay awake that long.'

'Me neither,' Aladdin said.

His father had tried to stay awake for the whole night in order to catch the thief, but it hadn't gone too well. He'd fallen asleep after just a few hours, and in the morning more food had disappeared. The following night his mother had stayed up, but she had nodded off even earlier than his father.

'Oh, for goodness' sake – you don't need to be awake at the same time,' Simona groaned. 'Think about it. Aladdin takes the first half of the night, then it's Billie's turn. Or vice versa.'

Billie didn't seem very keen on staying up half the night all on her own in the old tower. Aladdin felt the same.

'Well, what if we split the night into three?' Simona suggested. 'I could help you.'

After what had just happened in Mats's garden, Aladdin wasn't at all sure about this idea. What if everything went wrong again?

'We could use a whistle,' Billie said slowly. 'The person who's awake has a whistle around their neck, and if anyone comes along, we blow it.'

'What do we tell Mum and Dad?' Aladdin wondered.

'They don't need to know,' Simona said firmly. 'Just tell them Billie and I are coming for a sleepover.'

Actually, that wasn't a bad idea. They had already talked about a sleepover, but hadn't got round to it yet.

'OK,' Aladdin said. 'But not today. Let's see if any more food goes missing over the next week or so; if it does, we'll have to try and keep watch one night.'

'Cool!' Simona said. 'Well, no, obviously it's not cool, but it is exciting.'

Billie laughed, but Aladdin didn't. He was hoping that no more food would be stolen; he really didn't want to stay up, whether it was for the whole night or half the night.

'Something else occurred to me,' Billie said. 'Has food never gone missing before?'

'What do you mean?'

'I mean, it sounds as if this started a couple of weeks ago. Has it never happened before?'

'No,' Aladdin said. 'That is weird. Why didn't the thief take his chances before we sold the house and moved in?'

He tried to remember how long Mats had been working in the restaurant; it had to be several years. Why had he only started stealing food now?

Perhaps his parents were right; maybe the boy he had seen was a refugee, and he was the thief. The food had started to disappear around the time the boat arrived.

'By the way, why did you go round the back of Mats's house?' he asked Simona.

'I wanted to look through the windows to see if he was there.'

Billie almost choked on her juice. 'You're crazy,' she said.

'And did you see anything?' Aladdin wanted to know.

Simona twirled one of her long curls around her finger. 'No. Just two kids.'

Now it was Aladdin's turn to choke on his juice. 'What do you mean, kids?'

'Kids – ordinary kids.'

Aladdin shook his head. 'But that can't be right,' he said. 'Mats doesn't have any children.'

'They might not be his,' Simona said. 'Maybe they're just visiting.'

Aladdin thought hard. 'Did you see any adults in the house?'

'No, just the kids.'

'How old were they?' Billie asked.

Simona tilted her head on one side and considered the question. 'About our age, I guess.'

'What were they doing? Were they watching TV?' Aladdin wondered.

'I don't know. It was hard to see; the room was quite dark.'

'Dark?' Billie echoed.

'I saw them through one of the cellar windows. It looked as if they were sitting on the floor doing something – eating, maybe.' Simona reached for another biscuit. 'I didn't really think about what they were doing, but I remember thinking they looked a bit . . . different. Their clothes weren't like ours.'

'What do you mean?' Aladdin said.

'They looked kind of old. Perhaps they were hand-me-downs.'

Aladdin sat there in silence for a while. So there were two children in Mats's house. Two children he had never mentioned. Wearing strange clothes. But what puzzled Aladdin most was why they were sitting in the cellar, in a room that was 'quite dark'. It almost seemed as if they were hiding.

Chapter Seven

The restaurant was packed when Aladdin got home. Customers didn't usually turn up until later in the day, but now that it was winter, people seemed to like the idea of having dinner in the afternoon. He couldn't understand why his parents were having financial problems; the place was always busy.

Aladdin was still thinking about the children Simona had seen in the cellar, but most of all he was thinking about the fact that Mats had lied. He hadn't been visiting his mother at all. The question was, should he tell his parents right away? They wouldn't like the idea that Aladdin had been spying on Mats. Perhaps it was best to keep quiet about what they had been up to for a while longer.

He crept up to the kitchen. His parents didn't notice him as he pushed open the door. They were in the middle of a discussion, and they both looked angry.

'I think it's a terrible idea!' his mother said in a voice that Aladdin didn't recognize.

'Well, you come up with something better!' his father snapped.

'I already have! I want us to stay here and keep on fighting. We're not the only people in this country with financial problems right now, and it certainly wouldn't be any easier if we moved back to Turkey!'

Aladdin was so shocked that he forgot all about Mats. This was a hundred times worse. Move back to Turkey! He couldn't believe his ears. He never, ever wanted to leave Åhus.

His father reached out and stroked his mother's arm. Both of them looked sad now.

'I'm just saying it's an option we need to consider,' he said, sounding much calmer. 'We have to be realistic; we've got Aladdin to think about as well.'

Thank goodness – at least nothing had been decided. Not yet.

Aladdin quickly slipped out of the kitchen before they saw him. His heart was pounding so hard that it almost hurt. How short of money were they? He couldn't remember his parents ever talking about moving back to Turkey. What on earth would they do there? After all, they'd left in the first place because they didn't have a good life.

Aladdin ran down the stairs and took several deep breaths. He must keep an eye on his parents in future; they'd obviously been lying to him. Lying or not telling him the whole truth.

When he had calmed down, he went back up to the kitchen, trying to look as if he'd only just arrived home.

His mother was kneading dough; her face lit up when she saw him. 'Hello, sweetheart – have you had a good day?' she said.

'Yup,' Aladdin replied as he went over and stood beside her. 'What are you making?'

'Tear-and-share loaves; there were none left when we came in this morning.'

So the thief liked bread too.

Aladdin's mother put her arm around him, getting flour on his jumper. 'Tomorrow we're going to do something really nice,' she said. 'All three of us.'

The restaurant was closed on Sundays; Aladdin liked that. Things were much quieter.

His mother sighed. 'Oh no,' she said. 'The bulb's gone in the task light on my worktop. Could you run down to the cellar and fetch me a new one?'

Aladdin really wanted to go to his room to work on his latest model aeroplane. 'Can't you manage with the ceiling light?' he said.

'Not when I'm baking. I need to be able to see what I'm adding to the dough. Please, sweetheart?'

'All right,' Aladdin said reluctantly.

His mother stroked his face, covering his cheek with flour as well. 'You're such a good boy,' she said.

'Oh, Mum!'

She laughed. 'It's only a bit of flour, for goodness' sake!'

Aladdin wiped his cheek; a floury face wasn't a good look. He was just about to leave the kitchen when his mother stopped him.

'By the way, have you seen any more of that boy you mentioned?' She wasn't laughing now.

47

Aladdin shuffled uncomfortably. He really didn't want to talk about the boy. What if his mother mentioned the missing food? In that case he might have to tell her that he and Billie and Simona had been spying on Mats.

'No,' he said.

'Are you sure?'

'Yes. I haven't seen him since this morning.'

'When you ran outside in your socks?'

Aladdin blushed and nodded. He was embarrassed when he thought about how he had rushed out into the snow. It was definitely time to go down and fetch a light bulb, before his mother said any more.

He was just about to leave when he caught sight of the newspaper lying on the worktop. The leading article on the front page was about the refugee boat; the headline read: STILL NO PROSPECT OF A SOLUTION. But it was something else that had attracted his attention – a smaller article down below.

THE SILVER THAT DISAPPEARED, said the headline. Aladdin quickly read on:

Today it is exactly one hundred years since a bolt of lightning struck Larsson the silversmith's workshop in Åhus, and a quantity of silver was stolen. This silver has never been recovered. The question of who took it remains a mystery.

His father came into the kitchen before he had time to read any further.

'Leya, table three have changed their minds – they want the fish instead of the meatballs,' he said.

He opened the fridge and stuck his head inside. Aladdin's mother went over to help him, and they stood there jostling each other and laughing. They certainly didn't look cross any more. Aladdin's father had a special laugh that he only used when Mum was around. Billie had once said that Aladdin's parents seemed to be very much in love. He assumed that was a good thing – to be in love for such a long time. His mum and dad had known one another for ever.

They were so caught up with each other that they didn't notice Aladdin slip out of the kitchen. That business about moving back to Turkey must just have been something his father had come out with on the spur of the moment.

Chapter Eight

Aladdin ran all the way down the stairs, but when he reached the cellar door, he hesitated. He really didn't like going in there. But what could he do? Run back upstairs and ask his mum to come with him? No chance. And he was too old to be scared of going into the cellar on his own.

And anyway, how dangerous could it be?

He opened the door and set off down the steps. That was when he realized he'd forgotten to bring the torch. There was a ceiling light, but sometimes it switched itself off. His father had tried to fix it, but without success; the answer was to take a torch whenever you went down to the cellar.

Damn. Was he going to have to go all the way back up to the kitchen?

He looked up at the ceiling light. So far it seemed to be working perfectly well.

'I've got to stop being so scared,' he muttered to himself as he went down the last few steps.

Where on earth were the light bulbs? The cellar was quite large, and Aladdin edged his way carefully along. Why did his parents keep so much stuff? Wouldn't it be better to get rid of it? Or give it to someone who might like it? What was the point of having a cellar full of things you never used?

Besides which, the fact that the cellar was packed with all this rubbish made it much darker.

I'll just grab the light bulb, he thought; *then I'll get out of here.*

He picked up two large boxes that he thought might contain light bulbs. They didn't. Nor did the bags on the floor under one of the shelves.

Aladdin was just about to move another big box out of the way so that he could get past when he heard a noise behind him. It sounded as if someone was coming down the steps. The box slipped out of his hands and he whirled round.

There was no one there. 'Hello?' he said.

No reply.

51

Total silence.

Aladdin was really frightened now. If he could just find a light bulb, he would run back up to his room. He had no intention of setting foot in the cellar again for a very long time.

He picked up the box once more and moved it to one side; took a few steps and shifted another box. His hands were trembling and slippery with sweat.

There. Behind a large mirror on sturdy wooden legs was a shelf, and he could see several boxes of light bulbs. He tried to reach past the mirror, but annoyingly his arms weren't quite long enough. He would have to move the mirror.

He didn't have much time. He was sure he had heard someone coming down the steps. Someone who might still be in the cellar.

The mirror was big and heavy and covered in dust. Aladdin positioned himself in front of it so that he could get a good grip on the frame. It scraped against the floor as he dragged it out of the way.

At last! The light bulbs were within reach.

Just as he was about to pick one up, he happened to glance in the mirror. At first he saw only himself, but then he looked again and felt his heart stop.

Because the boy in the short trousers was standing behind him.

Aladdin let out a yell.

At which point the ceiling light switched itself off, and everything went black.

Chapter Nine

The darkness was like a thick blanket in front of Aladdin's eyes. He couldn't see a thing. All he could hear was his own rapid breathing. He had never been so scared in his entire life.

He didn't move a muscle. He waited and waited. His mum and dad would soon miss him; start wondering where he'd gone. If only they'd hurry up!

He couldn't hear a sound from the boy. What was he doing? Was he just standing there staring at Aladdin?

Aladdin opened his mouth to say something, but it was as if the fear had paralysed his throat. He tried a silent cough, which helped a bit.

'What do you want?' he said quietly, his voice trembling. 'Who are you?'

No reply.

'I know you're there,' Aladdin said, a little louder this time. 'I saw you in the mirror.'

His entire body was shaking as he turned round in the darkness. The boy still hadn't spoken.

If only he'd brought the torch. Aladdin swallowed hard several times. He was on the verge of tears. He tried putting both arms straight out in front of him; there was no one there.

He didn't dare start walking; what if he fell over some of the boxes and hurt himself? Suddenly he heard a crash at the other end of the room, and his heart leaped into his mouth. The boy must have knocked something over.

The ceiling light crackled, flashed a few times, then came back on. Aladdin was so relieved that he almost had to sit down. Instead he straightened up and looked around. There was no sign of the boy in the short trousers.

Aladdin had had enough. He raced up the cellar steps so fast that he didn't notice that someone else was halfway down.

He screamed in terror as he cannoned into a solid body.

'What on earth are you doing, Aladdin?'

It was only his dad.

Aladdin was so pleased to see him that he threw his arms around his neck. 'I . . . I . . .' he began, then hesitated. Should he tell his dad, or not? He might think Aladdin was making the whole thing up.

His dad stroked Aladdin's back, looking quite worried. He didn't usually get a big hug like this from his son these days.

'Let's go upstairs and have a chat,' he said.

Aladdin felt much better now that the light was on and he wasn't alone. He looked all around, but the boy was nowhere to be seen.

'I thought I saw the boy in the short trousers,' he said. 'You know, the boy I saw outside the restaurant.'

His father raised his eyebrows. 'Really? Your mum searched the tower earlier on, and she didn't find him. But perhaps he came in later?'

Looking closely at Aladdin, he gave a start. 'You're as white as a sheet!' he said anxiously. 'Were you really scared?'

Aladdin shuffled uncomfortably. 'I think it was more of a shock,' he mumbled.

His father folded his arms. 'What does he look like? I'm not happy with him creeping around in here and frightening people.'

Aladdin thought for a moment. 'He looks . . . serious,' he said. 'He never smiles or laughs. He almost seems angry. And he wears weird clothes.'

'You mean the wrong clothes for the time of year? That it's too cold for short trousers and just a jumper?'

Aladdin tried to remember exactly what the boy had looked like. Today he had been wearing a jacket, but there was something about him . . .

'I don't know about wrong,' he said. 'It's more that his clothes look so old. I don't know anyone who dresses like that.'

His father nodded slowly. He seemed to be thinking something over. 'Listen to me, Aladdin,' he said. 'Next time you see this boy, I want you to leave him alone.'

Aladdin was surprised. After all, he wasn't the one who had made contact with the boy; quite the reverse. It was the boy who kept seeking out Aladdin.

'I'm afraid that he might be having a hard time,' his father went on. 'He could be in real trouble. Perhaps he doesn't have proper clothes, or enough to eat. People who are in difficulties or afraid sometimes do silly things, and I don't want anything to happen to you. That's why I'm asking you to keep out of his way. It's better if your mum and I try to help him.'

How? Aladdin thought. *And with what?* The boy didn't say a word; he just came and went as he pleased. Besides which, Aladdin couldn't help feeling a bit annoyed at this talk of helping the boy; not long ago his father had said that they were so short of money they might have to go back to Turkey. In which case, how come they could afford to help the boy in the short trousers?

His father looked around. 'Now what was it I came down here for?' he laughed, scratching his forehead as he always did when he was trying to think. 'That's it – we need more serviettes. We've got new customers coming in as soon as someone gets up to leave.'

He found the serviettes in two seconds. Aladdin didn't understand how his father could find anything in the untidy cellar.

'I'm glad you met up with Billie and Simona today,' his father said. 'It's nice for you to have friends round when Mum and I are working such long hours.'

Aladdin's parents often said they felt guilty because he had to spend so much time on his own. His mother had once said she was sorry he didn't have any brothers or sisters. Aladdin thought it would have been nice to have a sibling, because then he would have had company all the time.

But then again, he wasn't really alone. Billie was also an only child; she could be Aladdin's sister when he needed one. Like tonight, for example.

They went back upstairs with the light bulb and the serviettes. Aladdin's legs still shook when he recalled how frightened he had been in the darkness. When he was back in his room, he remembered what his father had said about keeping out of the boy's way. But that wasn't exactly easy when he kept turning up.

Aladdin thought about the missing food. What if the thief really was Mats? Mum and Dad would be very disappointed in him – and angry too. If it was the boy in the short trousers, they would probably be less angry.

He sat down at his desk and started fiddling with one of his model planes. Perhaps Billie could come over and play a game. They could get something to eat from the restaurant and have supper in front of the TV. He put down the plane and picked up his phone, but Billie didn't answer. Typical. He'd have to call another friend instead.

For the first time in ages, Aladdin didn't want to be alone. All he could think about was the fact that they were running out of money, and that his father wanted to move back to Turkey. He just couldn't understand it, not even if his father had said it on the spur of the moment. He would just have to come up with a way of getting hold of more money. Otherwise they might have to leave Åhus.

Chapter Ten

The snow was beginning to melt and turn to slush. As he got ready for school on Monday, Aladdin dug out his yellow Wellingtons; he couldn't wear his ordinary winter boots, because they would be soaked through in no time.

He couldn't remember a weekend when so much had happened in such a short time. He almost felt as if he had dreamed the whole thing. It felt good to be going to school; perhaps everything would get back to normal!

When everyone had arrived, Aladdin's class teacher told them they would be working on a new topic: they would be finding out about the place where they lived.

'You don't know enough about Åhus,' Åsa said. 'And that's not right. It's important to know about your home town.'

Each pupil had to choose a place or a person they wanted to learn more about, she explained. Then they had to write a short piece about this place or person.

'I'd also like you to prepare a little presentation for the rest of the class.'

Aladdin sighed. He couldn't think of anyone or anywhere that he wanted to write about.

'Does the person have to be alive, or can we choose someone who's dead?' one of his classmates asked.

'It's absolutely fine if you want to write about someone who's dead,' Åsa said.

That didn't help Aladdin in the slightest. He would talk to his parents when he got home; perhaps they would have some ideas.

Then he remembered the newspaper article he had seen. What was it about again? Some old silver that had disappeared. Perhaps he could write about that.

Åsa came over. 'You look as if you're deep in thought,' she said.

Aladdin hesitated. Would it sound childish if he said he wanted to find out about the silver? After all, he hadn't even read the whole article. 'Well . . .' he said slowly. 'I'm a bit curious about that silversmith. The one whose silver went missing.'

To his surprise, Åsa's face lit up. 'What a wonderful idea, especially since you live in the old water tower!'

Aladdin hadn't a clue what she was talking about.

Åsa frowned. 'You do mean the silversmith in the article that was in the newspaper the other day?'

'Yes,' Aladdin said, sounding more sure of himself. 'But I didn't have time to read the whole piece . . .'

Åsa waved her hand. 'No problem, we can soon find it. This is going to be such fun. The silversmith's workshop used to be where the water tower is now.'

'Really?' Aladdin was completely taken aback.

'Really! But that was a very long time ago. The silversmith was very talented; people from all over Skåne wanted to buy the things he made.'

Aladdin hadn't known that either. 'What happened to him?' he asked.

'That's up to you to find out,' Åsa said.

'But you must be able to tell me something,' Aladdin persisted.

Åsa crouched down beside him. 'OK,' she said. 'I'll tell you one thing, but you have to find out the rest for yourself. Deal?'

Aladdin nodded.

'Good. This is what happened. As I said, the silversmith was very talented, and he was very hard-working. One night when he was working late, there was a terrible thunderstorm. A bolt of lightning struck one of the pine trees in his garden, and it came down on his workshop. He survived, but he had to leave, because the rain was hammering down. The following morning, when the storm had passed, he went back to his workshop, hoping to retrieve all the jewellery and bowls he had stored away. But guess what had happened . . .'

'They were gone?' Aladdin said.

'Exactly. Someone had been there during the night and stolen the lot. And the silversmith couldn't afford to buy more silver. He swore that he would find the thief, but he never did.'

'So no one knows who stole the silver?' Aladdin said.

'No. The police had their suspicions, but as the stolen goods were never found, there was nothing they could do.'

Åsa got to her feet. 'And now it's up to you to track down the rest of the story.' She winked at him and went off to help someone else.

Aladdin felt quite excited. He made a list of things he needed to find out. He would start by reading the newspaper article. An idea slowly began to take shape. Silver wasn't gold, but surely it must be worth quite a lot of money. Perhaps this school project would turn out to be very useful.

Chapter Eleven

Later that day, Aladdin met Billie down by the harbour. They wanted to see if the river was still frozen, but it wasn't. The mild weather had ruined the ice.

'That's a shame,' Billie said. 'I really wanted to go skating.'

It was dark outside, even though it was still the afternoon.

'Maybe it will freeze again at the weekend,' Aladdin said optimistically.

They sat down on one of the benches by the water and Aladdin told Billie about his new school project. He had called her as soon as he got home.

'I think it's cool that there used to be a silver-smith's workshop where your tower is now,' she said. 'I wonder what happened to all that stolen silver.'

That was exactly what Aladdin wanted to know.

His hat was making his head itch, so he took it off. The refugee boat was moored just a short distance away. He wondered what it was like for those living on board. He was used to sleeping on the water; every summer he and his parents moved onto their houseboat in the harbour. Although next summer things would be different, of course. The boat had been sold.

'You're very quiet,' Billie said.

Aladdin pulled his hat back on. Should he tell Billie how worried he was? Tell her he'd overheard his parents arguing, and that he was scared he'd have to leave Åhus? He took a deep breath, and it all just came out.

'I've got something to tell you,' he said. 'Let's go to Kringlan.'

Kringlan was a café on the square. The baker who owned it delivered bread to the Turk in the Tower, so sometimes Aladdin got free drinks and cakes there.

Billie ordered a cinnamon whirl and Aladdin some chocolate cake. When Aladdin told her what had happened, Billie started to cry.

'That's terrible,' she whispered.

Then Aladdin started to cry as well. A couple of elderly ladies at the next table were staring at them, so Aladdin and Billie quickly dried their eyes.

'Nothing's definite,' Aladdin said, prodding his cake. 'But I hate the fact that Dad has even mentioned going back to Turkey. I didn't know things were that bad.'

'But they haven't spoken to you? Asked you what you want to do?'

He shook his head.

'I don't get it,' Billie went on. 'I mean, are you even Turkish?'

Aladdin blinked. 'What? Yes, of course we are. Why wouldn't we be?'

Billie looked down at the table. 'Well, you've lived in Åhus for years and years. So doesn't that mean you're kind of Swedish?'

'I don't really think about whether I'm more Turkish or Swedish. It's a question of where I want to live, where I feel at home. And that's here, in spite of the fact that we speak Turkish and have Turkish relatives.'

'But would you be allowed to go back? I thought you said your dad had problems with the government or something.'

'It's different now. That's why we can go there on holiday and so on.'

They sat in silence for a while.

'Has any more food gone missing?' Billie said eventually.

It had. Aladdin had noticed that his parents were starting to get really angry.

'In that case we'll have to do what Simona suggested,' Billie said. 'See if we can keep watch all night at the weekend.'

'Mmm,' Aladdin said, taking a big bite of his cake.

Billie started giggling, even though she was still upset. 'As long as things don't go wrong like they did the other day when we were trying to spy on Mats,' she said.

'That wasn't much fun,' Aladdin said.

'Well, maybe a bit.' Billie giggled again. Then she became serious. 'It's not fair that food keeps disappearing,' she said. 'Not if you're so short of money that you might have to go back to Turkey. We have to do something. Soon.'

'I know. And I've got an idea.'

Billie's eyes widened. 'Tell me!'

Aladdin hesitated. 'I've been thinking about the silver I mentioned.'

Billie looked surprised. 'The silver that was stolen from the workshop?'

'Yes.'

'But hasn't it been missing for a really long time?' she said quietly.

'Well, yes,' Aladdin said.

He'd looked on the internet for information about the silversmith, but unfortunately he hadn't found very much. Not even the newspaper article. The silver had been stolen a hundred years ago. On the night the storm brought down the pine tree, the silversmith had had an unusually large amount of the precious metal in his workshop, because he'd received an order for several new items for the church in Åhus. Aladdin didn't know what all these items were, but among other things the silversmith was going to make a new baptismal font. Apparently it was a kind of bowl that the priest used when he was baptising babies.

Aladdin told Billie what he had found out.

'Wow,' she said. 'So you could almost say that the thief stole from the church.'

'Absolutely. The priest and the other people who worked for the church helped to search for the silver, but it was never found. The church even offered a reward for its return, but no one came forward. Apparently they had already paid the silversmith, so eventually they demanded their money back. But he had no money to give them.'

Billie took a bite of her cinnamon whirl. 'Maybe he stole the silver himself,' she said. 'Then claimed that someone else had done it.'

'That's what the police thought at first, but they couldn't prove it. And the silversmith stayed in Åhus, poor and alone. I don't think he would have done that if he was the thief; surely he would have moved away with all the silver. He would have bought a big house and eaten ice cream all day. Or something.'

'Weren't there any other suspects?' Billie wondered.

'Yes, but I can't find out his name. Or her name.'

'That doesn't matter,' Billie said firmly. 'He or she won't be around any more in any case.'

She was right, but Aladdin still wanted to know who the police believed had stolen the silver. Even if the thief was dead, he might still have relatives who were alive. What if there was a family here in Åhus who had a pile of stolen silver in their house?

'We ought to go and speak to someone in the church,' Billie said. 'They might know more about the smith and his silver.'

Aladdin smiled. 'We?'

'I want to come with you!'

'And are you going to help me write up my assignment for school as well?' Aladdin teased her.

'No chance,' Billie said. 'I just want to do the fun bits. Finding out information, that kind of stuff.' She laughed. 'Don't you want me to come?'

Aladdin grinned. Billie had quickly become one of his very best friends. He was happy to let her help him find out more about the missing silver. He really wished she would change her mind and transfer to his school; they could have had so much fun if they were in the same class.

'Of course I do,' he said.

Billie thought for a moment. 'Right,' she said. 'Let's do it. Let's try and find the silver, for real. I mean, it has to be somewhere. I'll help you; it must be worth a ton of money. Maybe you could sell it and stay in Åhus!'

For some strange reason Aladdin suddenly had a lump in his throat. 'We might not be able to keep the silver even if we do find it,' he said hoarsely.

'Whatever,' Billie said. 'We won't know that until we find it.' She looked at her watch. 'I have to be home in an hour; we've just got time to call in at the church before then. If we want to.'

'Let's go!' Aladdin said, leaping to his feet so quickly that his chair went crashing to the ground.

He had to do something to put an end to his mum and dad's problems. Finding the silver would be a good start.

It wasn't far to the church. They chatted and laughed as they crossed the square. Neither of them noticed the boy in the green trousers hiding round the corner of a building. He watched them closely, and nodded to himself as he realized they were heading for the church. When they had gone inside, he set off across the square. No one noticed him. And no one saw him sit down on the church steps, waiting.

Chapter Twelve

It was warm inside the church. Aladdin and Billie pulled off their woolly hats and gloves and unbuttoned their jackets. There was no sign of anyone else, not even the priest.

'What do we do now?' Billie asked.

'Let's take a walk around,' Aladdin suggested. 'There must be somebody here.'

They went round the pews and up to the altar. There was a piano at the front of the church; Billie sat down on the stool.

'You can play, can't you?' she said to Aladdin.

'Yes, but I'm not going to play now.'

'Why not?'

'Because it's not our piano. What if someone comes?'

74

Billie took a different view. 'If you play, maybe someone will come along and tell us where the priest is.' She got up from the stool.

Aladdin looked around. There wasn't a single person to be seen. Nor any ghosts . . . He sat down, still not convinced that this was a good idea.

'What shall I play?'

'Anything you like. Something nice.'

Something nice. Aladdin started to play a piece that his father had written; he had played it to Aladdin's mother at their wedding. As soon as he touched the keys, the notes echoed loudly throughout the empty church.

'Help!' he said, and stopped playing.

Billie laughed. 'Carry on and I'll dance!' she said.

Aladdin gave in. There was nobody around anyway. The music filled the church and they both got carried away. Billie danced around the font, giggling, and after only a couple of minutes they were having so much fun that they forgot where they were. Aladdin knew several tunes, and played one after the other. Billie's dancing grew wilder, and before long she was standing in the pulpit, waving her arms and legs. She looked like a jumping jack.

All of a sudden they heard a deep voice:

'You two seem to be having a good time.'

Billie was so scared that she almost fell down the pulpit steps. Aladdin immediately stopped playing and stood up. Neither of them had seen the priest emerge from a door in the corner of the church. Thank goodness he didn't look angry; in fact, he was smiling.

'You play very well,' he said to Aladdin. 'You should come along and play at one of our services.' He looked at Billie. 'And perhaps you could dance for us.'

Billie blushed, while Aladdin hoped the priest was joking. There was no way he could play in front of a whole load of people!

'We couldn't find anybody,' he said. 'I mean, we came here to speak to you, but we couldn't see you.'

'So you started to play the piano instead,' the priest said. 'You did the right thing. I wish more people would come in here and spread a little joy.' He looked from one to the other. 'So how can I help you?'

It wasn't easy to explain, but Aladdin did his best. He told the priest about the school project, and what he had learned about the silversmith.

'Aha,' the priest said. 'So it's your parents who own the Turk in the Tower. An excellent restaurant – I often eat there.'

Billie came down from the pulpit to join Aladdin. 'Did you know about the silversmith?' she asked.

'Indeed I did,' the priest replied. 'There's a lot to tell. That poor man – he was sorely tested.'

He suddenly looked sad. 'But he wasn't the only one who had problems when the silver disappeared. I presume you've heard that a man here in the village was accused of being the thief?'

Aladdin and Billie nodded, but they still didn't know who the man was.

'It was such a mess,' the priest went on. 'Listen, I don't have time to talk to you about all this right now; I have to get ready for a funeral. Could you come back tomorrow at the same time?'

They certainly could. On the way out Aladdin cast a final glance at the piano, and reminded himself that he needed to start practising again.

It had started to snow. Big, heavy flakes were falling from the sky, covering the ground like a thick white blanket. Aladdin pulled his hat well down.

'I think I'd better go home,' Billie said.

'Me too,' Aladdin agreed.

They decided to meet outside the church at the same time the following day. Billie waved and ran off, while Aladdin set off in the opposite direction.

Only then did he notice the boy on the steps.

He stopped and stood there as if he had been turned to stone. There was no one around; Billie had already crossed the road and turned onto another street.

The boy gazed silently at Aladdin, who thought he looked angry. His mouth was dry with fear. He didn't dare move a muscle.

The boy got up and walked away.

Aladdin wasn't sure what to do. He remembered all too clearly how frightened he had been in the cellar, and he was frightened now. But his curiosity got the better of him. He ran after the boy, who went round the corner of the church and disappeared into the darkness.

Aladdin stopped dead.

Into the darkness. Just like in the cellar.

His heart was pounding again. He had no desire to run around in a dark churchyard. The outcome was always the same: the boy vanished and Aladdin couldn't find him.

Slowly he turned round. It was when he reached the front of the church that he got the feeling something was wrong. He stood there alone in the melting snow and stared at the steps. What was bothering him?

Eventually he realized what it was. The boy had left no impression in the snow. Not on the step where he had been sitting, nor where he had walked round the church. Aladdin couldn't believe his eyes. He edged closer; he was so nervous that he was holding his breath.

He could clearly see his own footprints.

But there was no trace of the boy.

Chapter Thirteen

Aladdin found it difficult to get to sleep that night. He couldn't stop thinking about the boy. How could he walk through the snow without leaving footprints?

Just before midnight he gave up and switched on his bedside light. If he read for a little while, perhaps he would be able to sleep.

That was when he heard something on the stairs. The sound of footsteps.

He froze.

The food thief was back!

Aladdin was so scared that he didn't even dare to switch off the light and wriggle down. He just kept thinking that there was a thief coming up the stairs, and there was no lock on his bedroom door.

His parents had gone to bed over an hour ago. What if something happened to Aladdin, and they didn't hear?

He sat there motionless, his heart beating so fast that he could hear a rushing sound in his ears.

Then he heard a voice speaking quietly:

'I was sure I'd forgotten to lock the front door.'

Aladdin let out a huge sigh of relief. It was his dad's voice. Soon he heard more footsteps; his mum, of course.

'Ssh, you'll wake Aladdin,' she whispered.

'No I won't,' his dad said, although he had lowered his voice.

Then Aladdin heard his name mentioned again:

'It's obvious that Aladdin has something on his mind,' his mother said.

'He's probably thinking about that business of the stolen silver,' his father said.

Aladdin slid out of bed without making a sound and tiptoed over to the door.

'It's more than that,' his mother said. 'I've been thinking about that refugee boy who has been hanging around the tower. Aladdin hasn't mentioned him today. Perhaps they've become friends, and are seeing each other more regularly, but Aladdin doesn't want to tell us about it.'

What? Had she gone crazy? Why would Aladdin keep something like that a secret?

'Hmm,' his father said. 'Not that it matters – Aladdin can be friends with whoever he likes. But that doesn't really sound like him. He doesn't usually hide things from us.'

There was a faint creak from the staircase as his mother moved.

'But *we're* hiding things from *him*,' she said.

Aladdin's stomach tied itself in a knot of fear.

'You mean our financial problems? Aladdin understands more than we think – and we have talked openly about it. Well, to a certain extent,' his father said.

'I mean the idea of moving back to Turkey,' his mother said. 'Shouldn't we discuss it with him?'

Now there was a lump of ice in Aladdin's stomach. Had everything already been arranged? Could they really do such a thing?

His father's reply reassured him:

'Nothing's definite – best not to worry him unnecessarily. Anyway, I thought you didn't want to move. That's what it sounded like the other day.'

'I've given it a lot of thought,' his mother said slowly. 'You're right – it might be easier for us to open a restaurant in one of the tourist resorts.'

It sounded as if she was heading up the stairs now.

'But if I go with my heart, I'd rather stay here in Åhus,' she added.

It sounded as if she was crying, and Aladdin went cold all over. Should he just open the door to let them know he had heard what they were saying?

But something held him back. As he edged away from the door, he heard his father consoling his mother.

'Leya, we don't have to move tomorrow. We've still got time to turn this around.'

They headed on up the stairs, and silence descended once more.

Aladdin got back into bed and pulled the covers right up to his chin. It was a good job Billie wasn't there, because otherwise they would both have started crying again. His father had said they had time, but not how much. Suddenly Aladdin felt as if finding the stolen silver was more urgent than ever.

This has to work, he thought. *It doesn't matter if the silver has been missing for a thousand years. I'm going to find it. Whatever it takes.*

Chapter Fourteen

Aladdin didn't know how it happened, but at long last he fell asleep. Perhaps it was because his mother had said she didn't want to move. Not if she had a choice.

The following morning it was cold again, as if the weather couldn't make up its mind. His mother made him put on two pairs of gloves before he dashed off to school.

His teacher was very pleased when he told her that he and Billie had been to the church.

'We're going back this afternoon,' he said proudly.

'How exciting – well done!' Åsa said. 'By the way, I've got something for you.'

She went over to her desk and picked up a thin book. 'There you go,' she said, handing it to Aladdin.

He looked at the book and frowned. 'What's it about?'

'Silversmiths in Sweden,' Åsa said. 'I found it in the library yesterday. Your silversmith is in there, if you want to know more about him.'

The book was as light as a feather in Aladdin's hand.

He just couldn't wait for the school day to end so that he could rush over to the church. Two hours still to go. Åsa had said that they would be working on their Åhus projects, so he might as well read the chapter about his silversmith right away. Perhaps it would make the time pass more quickly.

The smith had been a lonely man. He had always lived in a little house just a stone's throw from his workshop. He had no family. His work had been the most important aspect of his life, and the night the lightning struck the pine tree, everything was destroyed. The workshop was ruined and the silver disappeared, just as Aladdin had already heard.

His eyes widened as he read on, because according to the book, the silversmith had gone mad when he lost his livelihood. He was angry with everything and everyone, and started to behave badly towards other people. Eventually the whole village was afraid of him. The police came and took him away to a mental hospital. Apparently this was a place for people who were so unwell that they could be a danger to themselves or others.

No one heard from the silversmith after that. He died in the hospital a few years later. According to the book, lots of messages were found under the mattress of his hospital bed.

Quickly Aladdin took out his notebook so that he could jot down the questions he wanted to ask the priest.

As long as he was concentrating on the silversmith's story, it was easy to avoid thinking about more difficult matters. Such as the fact that he couldn't work out how the boy in the short trousers could walk through the snow without leaving any footprints.

I must have been mistaken, Aladdin thought. *It was dark and it was snowing when we came out of the church; I must have been mistaken*.

He carried on making notes.

*

They met on the church steps after school, the building looming above them like a huge dark shadow. Aladdin looked for the boy in the short trousers, but there was no sign of him.

'Who are you looking for?' Billie asked.

'Nobody.' Aladdin didn't want to tell Billie that he had seen the boy again; instead he told her what he had found out from the book Åsa had given him.

'This is great,' Billie said. 'We've got to find that silver, and fast! Or we need to come up with another way of earning money. Has any more food gone missing, by the way?'

'Not last night, no.'

'Perhaps it's over,' Billie said optimistically.

'Perhaps.'

Billie smiled. 'You know what we said: if it carries on, me and Simona will help you catch the thief at the weekend.'

The thief . . . If it was the boy who was taking food, Aladdin didn't think it was right to call him a thief.

'Maybe it isn't a real thief,' he said.

'Of course it is.'

'Not if the person who's taking the food is doing it because he or she is hungry.'

'What are you talking about? You can't just steal stuff because you're hungry!'

'Hmm,' Aladdin said. 'Come on, let's go inside.'

He pulled open the church door and slipped into the warmth. The notebook containing his list of questions was under his arm. He kept thinking about the notes under the silversmith's mattress.

They had all said the same thing: *It was Orvar who took the silver.*

But who was Orvar?

Chapter Fifteen

'Orvar was the silversmith's arch-enemy,' the priest explained.

They were sitting in a row in the front pew, right by the altar, with the priest in the middle. Today there were candles burning in the sconces along the walls, their glow casting shadow patterns on the white surface; patterns that almost looked like ghosts.

Aladdin couldn't help shuddering.

'Orvar and the silversmith were in love with the same girl, you see,' the priest went on. 'They pursued her for several years before she finally made up her mind: she wanted to marry the silversmith, not Orvar.'

'But the book I read said that the silversmith was all alone,' Aladdin objected.

'That's true. Or to put it more accurately, he ended up all alone. His fiancée fell ill the week before the wedding. She died before they could get married.'

'Oh no – that's terrible!' Billie said, her eyes shining with tears.

'Indeed it was,' the priest said. 'And things got worse, because Orvar claimed it was the silver-smith's fault. If he had taken care of the girl, she wouldn't have died. That was just poisonous gossip, of course; she died of pneumonia, and that was no one's fault. But neither the silversmith nor Orvar ever got over it.'

'So what happened next?' Aladdin said impatiently.

'The two of them remained enemies. Orvar found another girl to marry, but the silversmith never did. When the workshop was destroyed, he had nothing left. He had lost his love and his job. That was when he lost his mind too, and ended up in the mental hospital.'

Lost his mind. It sounded dreadful.

'Did anyone else think that it was Orvar who had taken the silver?' Billie asked.

'Oh yes,' the priest said. 'The police were convinced he was the thief, but they could never prove it. The silver was gone, and they couldn't lock Orvar up without evidence.'

'Although it sounds as if that's what he deserved,' Aladdin said. He felt angry when he thought about Orvar, who seemed to have ruined the silversmith's life.

The priest placed a hand on Aladdin's shoulder. 'Don't judge Orvar too harshly,' he said. 'He suffered his share of misery too.'

'Serves him right,' Aladdin muttered.

The priest looked sad. 'The silversmith lost his workshop,' he said, 'but Orvar lost his whole family. If he really was the one who took the silver, then he was severely punished, even though the police couldn't do anything.'

'What happened?' Billie asked.

But Aladdin broke in before the priest had time to answer.

'What do you think? Do you think Orvar was the thief?'

The priest laughed. 'How could I possibly know that? All this happened such a long time ago.'

'Could it have been the silversmith himself?' Billie wondered.

The priest lowered his eyes. 'That's exactly what we don't know,' he said. 'The thing is, there was never any real evidence against Orvar. And we know that the silversmith hated him. Perhaps he took the silver and hid it so that he could blame his enemy and ruin his life. Perhaps the silversmith was already having some mental health issues before the silver went missing, but no one had noticed. People who are unwell sometimes do strange things.'

They sat in silence for a little while. Aladdin tried to sum up what they had learned from the priest.

They were no closer to knowing what had happened to the silver, but it seemed pretty clear that the thief was either Orvar or the silversmith himself.

Orvar or the silversmith . . . How could they find out?

Then he thought about the question Billie had asked before he interrupted. 'You said Orvar lost his whole family. What happened?'

'Orvar married a woman from a neighbouring village,' the priest said. 'I think her name was Elvira. She and Orvar had two sons. One day she sent the elder boy off on an errand, but he never came home; he died in an accident. His mother was so devastated that she left Orvar. She took their younger son, and she never came back. I think she moved to Kristianstad to be with her mother. Orvar was left all alone in Åhus with his dog.'

Billie picked up a hymn book from the shelf in front of her. 'So he wasn't completely alone,' she said. 'Not if he had a dog.'

'You could look at it that way, I suppose,' the priest said. 'But if you've had a wife and children, I don't think a dog would be enough, somehow.'

He shuffled on the hard wooden pew. 'Well, I'm afraid that's just about all I can tell you.'

'Is there anyone who might know about the actual police investigation?' Aladdin wondered. 'A former police officer who might have been involved?'

'I very much doubt it,' the priest said with a smile. 'Anyone who was on the case would be over a hundred years old today.'

He got to his feet, then quickly sat down again. 'Although there is one person you could talk to – an elderly lady who helps out here in the church.

Her name is Elsa. She looks after our archive, and I'm sure she'd be able to show you some pictures of Orvar and the silversmith. Would that help?'

Aladdin and Billie nodded eagerly; that would be great!

'Good. In that case I'll ring her and find out when she's available.'

'Brilliant!' Aladdin said.

'I'll be in touch when I've spoken to her,' the priest said.

He stood up again, a knowing smile playing around his lips. 'Just don't let her frighten the life out of you with her stories. She believes in ghosts and all kinds of strange things. And if she starts talking about the Silver Boy, promise me you won't take any notice, because it's all nonsense.'

'The Silver Boy?' Aladdin echoed in surprise.

'It's just an old tale,' the priest said evasively.

'About what?' Aladdin persisted.

The priest hesitated. 'About another child who really wanted to find the silver,' he said. 'A child who died a very long time ago.'

Chapter Sixteen

The priest called that very same evening. The lady who helped out in the church wasn't very well, but would be happy to meet them the following week. This was later than Aladdin had hoped, but there was nothing he could do about it. They needed all the help they could get, and he really wanted to hear more about the Silver Boy.

He soon had something else to think about. More food went missing from the kitchen. His parents discussed the idea of installing a camera, but it would take time to sort that out – maybe another week.

Aladdin rang Billie and Simona.

'See you at the weekend then,' Simona said. 'On Saturday evening. You'll see – we'll soon put a stop to your food thief!'

She made it sound so simple, but Aladdin wasn't convinced.

However, he still couldn't wait for Saturday. His parents were working so hard that he hardly saw them. In one way that was good; they were definitely too busy to start planning a move to Turkey.

At last the week was over. Aladdin finished off one of his model planes while he was waiting for Billie and Simona to arrive, then he went down to the cellar to fetch the inflatable mattresses for his guests. He ran down and back up again, but this time he was left in peace; no one scared him while he was in the storeroom.

'This is nice,' his mother said when she walked past his room and saw him making up the beds. She looked very tired. 'I'm glad you've got some company tonight.' And she hurried away.

Aladdin remembered when he was little: back then his parents had always made sure they didn't both work at the weekends; one of them was always free to play with him. It made him sad when he thought about it; things had changed without his even noticing.

Billie and Simona arrived at six o'clock, as agreed. As usual, Simona had brought her big rucksack, while Billie was carrying a bag full of books. What was she going to do with them? Hit the thief over the head?

'When does the thief usually strike?' she asked.

'How am I supposed to know that?' Aladdin said. 'If I knew that, we could have caught him weeks ago.'

'Right,' Billie sighed. 'I was just checking whether we really have to stay up all night.'

They collected some food from the restaurant and sat down on the sofa to eat. Simona told a story about something silly her father had done; Billie laughed, but Aladdin wasn't really listening. He just wanted the time to pass so that they could put their plan into action. At the weekend he was allowed to stay up as late as he liked, but his parents would probably be a bit surprised if they didn't go to bed at all.

'Well, of course we're going to go to bed,' Simona said. 'Otherwise we'll never cope.'

'So where is the person who's awake going to be?' Billie wondered. 'Upstairs in the restaurant?'

Aladdin had given the matter some thought. The restaurant closed at ten, and by eleven his parents would have finished the cleaning and the washing-up. By then they were tired, and usually went straight to bed.

'We need to wait until Mum and Dad are asleep,' he said. 'Then the person who's keeping watch can sneak up to the restaurant.'

He wasn't sure if they were going to be able to see it through. Who wanted to sit all alone in a dark restaurant for hours on end, waiting for a thief?

He could tell that Billie was thinking the same thing. As usual, Simona wasn't scared of anything, but Aladdin thought she might change her mind when she was sitting there in the darkness.

Then he had an idea.

'We could sleep up there,' he said. 'All three of us. When Mum and Dad have gone to bed, we take our mattresses up to the restaurant. Two of us can sleep while the other one keeps watch; that means none of us will be alone.'

Simona fiddled with the whistle she had brought with her; it was the kind that can be attached to a lifejacket, and it was incredibly loud.

'That means we'd definitely hear if someone blows the whistle,' she said.

Which was also a good thing. It would be terrible if someone was up there all alone blowing the whistle, and no one came.

'We need to be careful,' Aladdin warned the girls. 'We mustn't blow the whistle unless we're absolutely certain that the thief is there. If Mum and Dad wake up and find us in the restaurant, they'll be furious.'

'But we do have to wake them if the thief turns up?' Billie said anxiously.

'Yes, of course,' Aladdin said. 'But not otherwise.'

'What if the thief doesn't show up?' Simona asked.

'In that case we just need to bring the mattresses back down here before Mum and Dad wake up,' Aladdin said, leaning back on the sofa. At last they had a plan.

'I've been thinking about those kids who might be living in Mats's cellar,' Simona said after a while.

Aladdin had completely forgotten about them. There had been so many other things in his head.

'Why?' Billie said.

Simona shook her head. 'I don't really know. There was something about the way they were sitting on the floor. And their clothes. I was wondering whether . . .'

'What?' Aladdin said.

'Oh, nothing. I just thought they looked kind of lonely. Forget it – let's concentrate on catching whoever has been stealing your food.'

On that particular evening the restaurant stayed open longer than usual; it was eleven o'clock before Aladdin's mother came down to say goodnight.

'It's lovely and cosy in here,' she said as she popped into Aladdin's room.

All three of them were in their pyjamas, sitting up in bed. Just as if they were about to go to sleep.

'Mmm,' Aladdin said.

His mother kissed him on the forehead, as she always did last thing at night. 'Don't stay awake for too long,' she said.

When she had gone back upstairs, they were all quiet for a little while.

'I hope it won't take them long to do the washing-up,' Simona said with a yawn. 'I'm really tired.'

'Why don't you go to sleep for a little while?' Aladdin said. 'Billie and I will wake you up when it's time, and you can take the first shift.'

So that was settled. It was almost midnight by the time they were sure Aladdin's parents had gone to sleep; just to be on the safe side, he tiptoed up to their bedroom and listened outside the door.

'They're definitely asleep,' he said to Billie when he got back.

They woke Simona and made their way up to the restaurant. It was difficult to negotiate the narrow staircase with their mattresses, pillows and duvets. For the hundredth time Aladdin thought that keeping watch all night probably wasn't such a good idea. What if Mum and Dad found them? Or what if the thief actually turned up? The very thought made him feel quite ill.

Eventually they made it. They had to move several tables to make room for two mattresses; it felt very odd, lying on the floor with furniture all around them.

'As long as my dad doesn't decide to get up and check everything's OK in the middle of the night,' Aladdin whispered.

'No chance,' Simona whispered back. 'Didn't you hear him snoring when we went past their bedroom?'

'You won't fall asleep, will you?' Aladdin said to her. 'If you feel tired, wake me or Billie.'

'I will,' Simona promised.

'Who are you going to wake first?' Billie asked, sitting up.

'You. Aladdin can take the last shift and decide when it's time to go back to his room.'

That sounded sensible. They had to be out of the restaurant before Aladdin's parents woke up.

'You're not scared, are you?' Simona hissed to Billie.

Aladdin looked over at Billie. She was as white as a sheet.

'Maybe a bit,' she whispered as she lay down.

They didn't want to turn on the main light, so they had brought torches. They switched them off, and the room was in darkness. That was good; the thief wouldn't be able to see them on the floor behind all the tables.

They agreed that the person who was keeping watch would sit in a corner right by the door. After a while their eyes grew accustomed to the darkness, and they could at least make out the shapes of the tables and chairs.

'Is it OK to read by torchlight?' Billie asked.

'No,' Simona said. 'If you do that, the thief will be able to tell that there's someone in the restaurant.'

'Of course.'

Billie closed her eyes as tightly as she could and turned over. Simona settled down in the corner.

Aladdin lay awake for a long time, twisting and turning. He was never going to be able to get to sleep. This was far too exciting. He glanced over at Billie; she was fast asleep, her breathing slow and even. Aladdin sighed. He couldn't hear a sound from Simona. He hoped she hadn't nodded off.

He sat up and looked in her direction, but he couldn't see her. He stood up, and then he saw her. She was staring at the door and the stairs, not moving a muscle.

He felt reassured, and lay down again. He might as well rest, otherwise he wouldn't be able to manage his shift.

He had barely finished forming the thought when he fell asleep.

Chapter Seventeen

Aladdin was in a deep sleep, as if he'd been awake for a thousand hours.

Billie shook him. Hard. 'It's your turn now,' she whispered.

She was so tired that Aladdin hardly had time to move before she lay down on his mattress.

'Did you see anything?' he asked.

'Not a thing. Neither did Simona.'

'But you did stay awake?'

Billie felt a spurt of anger. 'Of course I did!'

She hesitated. 'But it's horrible, sitting there all alone in the dark. It's a good job we all decided to sleep up here, otherwise I would never have stayed!'

With that she lay down and fell asleep right away.

Aladdin went over and sat down in the corner. From the restaurant's location at the top of the tower, you could see the whole of Åhus. There were hardly any lights on; it looked as if the whole village was sleeping. Apart from Aladdin. It was just as Billie had said: he felt alone, even though he had company.

Aladdin couldn't help thinking about the boy in the short trousers. What was he up to, running around hiding in people's cellars? Why? What did he want? Didn't he realize that it wasn't OK to do that kind of thing?

He shuffled about so that he was almost lying down, leaning against the wall. It was quiet and peaceful. Actually, it wasn't all that quiet. Aladdin kept hearing noises – from the freezer in the kitchen, from the wind whistling outside the window. He drew up his knees and wrapped his arms around them. He didn't know whether he wanted the thief to turn up or not. He had the whistle around his neck; if anyone came, Aladdin would blow the whistle as hard as he could.

He tried to resist, but he could feel himself getting drowsier by the minute. The darkness didn't exactly help; the only thing keeping him awake was fear. Several times he suddenly realized he had his eyes closed, but whenever he thought he heard a noise, he gave a start.

'I have to stay awake,' he whispered to himself. 'I mustn't fall asleep.'

But eventually he lost the battle. In spite of the fact that he was as taut as a violin string, Aladdin nodded off with his head resting against the wall, the whistle around his neck.

He dreamed that he could hear a noise. It was faint, and it only lasted for a short while. Then he heard it again; it was still faint, but it sounded as if it had moved closer. He thought it was coming from the stairs. Yes, definitely the stairs. It was the clear sound of footsteps.

In spite of the fact that he was asleep, he started fumbling for the whistle.

You have to wake up, he thought. *Wake up, Aladdin!*

The footsteps were so light that it couldn't possibly be Mats.

Aladdin didn't know whether he was awake or dreaming, but fear sent a chill down his spine.

There was someone standing in the doorway, wasn't there?

Aladdin blinked, over and over again.

Yes, there was definitely someone there.

It was the boy in the short trousers. He stood there for a long time, staring at Aladdin.

He was wearing exactly the same clothes as on the first two occasions when Aladdin had seen him: green trousers and a striped jumper. Long socks and boots.

The boy looked down at the floor, a sad expression on his face.

Aladdin's heart was pounding.

Then the boy spoke for the first time. 'You have to help me,' he whispered. 'You have to find the silver that disappeared from the workshop.'

Aladdin's jaw dropped. He was incapable of making a sound.

'You have to find the silver,' the boy repeated. 'Talk to Ella. She knows.'

Then he vanished.

Just as quickly as he had appeared.

*

A second later, Aladdin woke with a start. Simona was shaking his arm.

'You have to be the worst spy in the world,' she said crossly.

Billie was rushing around trying to gather all their things together. 'We need to get back downstairs,' she said. 'Quickly, before your parents wake up.'

Aladdin could hardly remember where he was; then it all came back to him and he leaped to his feet. He had dreamed about the boy. What was it he'd said? He'd talked about the silver. And about someone called Ella.

'The food,' he mumbled.

'We've already checked,' Billie said. 'Nothing has been taken.'

That was a relief. Aladdin was really ashamed of having fallen asleep. Quietly they carried the mattresses and bedding downstairs.

Aladdin couldn't stop thinking about his dream. His mother always said that we dream about things we've done or things that are on our mind, so it was hardly surprising that Aladdin had dreamed about the silver and the boy in the short trousers.

But Ella . . . why had he dreamed about someone called Ella?

And why did he recognize the name?

Chapter Eighteen

Billie and Simona went home after breakfast.

'You all seem very tired,' Aladdin's mother said as they stood in the hallway putting on their coats. 'Didn't you sleep well?'

They looked at one another and giggled. No, they hadn't slept well. Billie and Simona had been teasing Aladdin because he had nodded off.

'No. I don't think any of us did,' Simona said.

Aladdin had no excuses; he just hadn't been able to stay awake. He had decided not to tell them about his dream, where the boy in the short trousers had spoken and asked Aladdin for his help.

He shook his head. A dream was a dream, and nothing else, but the fact that the boy had mentioned the name Ella stuck in his mind.

He locked the door when Billie and Simona had left. They didn't usually bother during the day, but Aladdin felt safer with it locked.

As he set off up the stairs back to his room, it suddenly struck him: Ella was the old lady who had helped him and Billie when they were trying to catch the ghost in Billie's house! Ella had lived in Åhus for a long, long time. Aladdin felt a great wave of relief. It wasn't so strange that Ella had turned up in his dream after all! He had been wondering whether the boy might be a ghost, and Ella was a real gossip who believed in ghosts and restless spirits.

Aladdin sat down on the sofa and started to work on one of his model aeroplanes. He was soon interrupted by his mother.

'Guess what – nothing was stolen last night,' she said.

'Good.'

'Who knows – maybe whoever was taking the food is full now!' his mother said with a wink.

'Maybe.'

The thief had come almost every night over the past week. So why hadn't he come last night, when

Aladdin and his friends were keeping watch in the restaurant?

Or perhaps he had come, and they hadn't noticed? Perhaps he had been there when Aladdin was asleep, and had run away when he realized he wasn't alone? Or was the boy in the short trousers the thief? Could it be that Aladdin hadn't been dreaming after all?

His father came into his room. 'Maybe things are looking up,' he said.

Aladdin gazed at his parents. They looked so tired. Had they been working extra hard over the last week? Or was it because of their money worries? He suddenly felt very lonely. Why didn't they tell him what was going on? Trying to guess was much, much worse.

'I think we should have some fun today,' his mother said. 'All three of us. What do you think? What would you like to do?'

Aladdin was so tired he could hardly keep his eyes open, but he made an effort to look pleased. It didn't really work.

'Aren't you feeling well, Aladdin?' his father said anxiously, placing a hand on his forehead.

Aladdin twisted his head aside. 'I'm fine,' he said. 'What shall we do?'

'We could drive down to Kivik,' his mother suggested. 'There's a fantastic hill for sledging!'

'Good idea,' his father said. 'We can have lunch there too.'

Sledging was the last thing Aladdin felt like doing, but on the other hand he really wanted to get away from the tower and the restaurant for a while. His parents must have felt the same, because they were ready in no time. A few minutes later they were in the car. His father switched on the radio as his mother pulled out of the car park. The local news was on, and the newsreader was talking about the refugee boat in the harbour.

'I really don't want to hear this at the moment,' his father said, and turned off the radio.

Aladdin leaned back against the headrest. He could have a little sleep in the car, then he would feel brighter when they arrived. As they turned onto the main road, he automatically glanced back at the tower. His stomach flipped over. A boy wearing a jacket and short trousers was sitting on the steps, staring at their car. Aladdin was about to tell his parents when he noticed something that made him change his mind.

The boy on the steps was crying.

It was dark when they got back from Kivik. His parents were really happy, chatting and laughing. Aladdin felt better too; it had been a good day.

The steps were empty when they got out of the car. Of course. The boy wouldn't have hung around any longer than necessary. It was a good job Aladdin hadn't said anything to his parents.

'I'm hungry!' his mother said as she ran up the stairs to the kitchen. 'I'm going to make us a delicious supper!'

His father went down to the cellar, but reappeared after less than a minute. Aladdin had only just had time to take off his shoes.

'Ha!' his father said. 'Come with me – I've got something to show you!'

He practically dragged Aladdin down the cellar steps.

'I don't know why I didn't think of it before,' he said. He walked across the cellar to the outside wall. Half hidden behind an old bookcase was a door. Aladdin couldn't remember ever having seen it before.

'It's a fire door,' his father explained. 'I've always thought it was jammed shut, because it's so old and rusty. But look what happens when I try the handle.'

He pushed down on it, and the door opened easily.

'Do you think the thief got in this way?' Aladdin said.

'Absolutely.'

'But it doesn't open very far, because the bookcase is in the way. He must be a very small thief, in that case!'

'That's true,' his father said. 'What do you think? Could the boy you've seen get in through there?'

Aladdin looked at the gap. Cold air poured in and made him shiver. He nodded slowly. 'I think he could,' he said quietly.

Why did he feel as if he was betraying the boy? Maybe he was just hungry . . .

'Good,' his father said. 'In that case I'll make sure this door is kept locked in future.'

He glanced at Aladdin. 'Don't worry about the boy,' he said. 'We'll leave a bag of food out for him tonight, then we'll see whether he takes it, or if that's an end to all the nocturnal visits.'

That made Aladdin feel better. A bag of food sounded good. Now it was just a matter of waiting to see if anyone came and took it.

Chapter Nineteen

And they did. The food his father left on the steps disappeared. His mother decided it must have been the boy in the short trousers who had taken it. They agreed that they would carry on leaving food out for him – at least, as long as the refugees were still living on the boat in the harbour.

The newspapers were publishing more and more articles about the refugee boat. People were starting to get angry because it had been there for such a long time. Aladdin couldn't understand it; after all, the refugees weren't doing any harm. They were just sitting there on board, waiting. Waiting to be given permission to stay in Sweden. In school he had learned that the refugees were from Syria. Åsa, his teacher, explained that they had travelled right across Europe by lorry, then by boat across the Baltic Sea to Åhus. Had they come all this way just to be sent back home? Aladdin wondered.

'At least that's solved one of our problems,' his father said on the third evening after he had put out the bag of food. He looked at Aladdin's mother with a sorrowful expression.

Aladdin felt the same. It was good that the thief was no longer getting in, of course, but it wasn't enough to save the restaurant. Aladdin realized that.

The priest rang him on Monday evening. The lady he and Billie were going to speak to was feeling better. Aladdin was relieved; he just had to find the silver, and perhaps the old lady would know where it was. The priest suggested they should meet at the Kringlan café the very next day. The lady would bring some photographs, as the priest had suggested. Aladdin thought that sounded good; Billie would be able to come too. He was just about to hang up when he thought of something.

'Sorry,' he said. 'What was the lady's name again? Was it Elsa?'

'No, it's not Elsa. But I might have said the wrong thing, because our cantor's name is Elsa. The lady you're going to meet is Ella.'

Aladdin almost dropped the phone. 'Ella?' he whispered.

'That's it. By the way, she was sure she'd met you and Billie before – could that be true?'

Aladdin swallowed. 'I think it could,' he said quietly.

It was just as the boy in the dream had said: *Talk to Ella. She knows.*

Just as Aladdin thought things were improving slightly, they got worse. Much worse.

He had brushed his teeth and was on his way to bed. Usually he could hear sounds from the restaurant, but this evening it was unusually quiet in the tower. His father was sitting on his bed waiting for him when he got back from the bathroom.

'What's up?' Aladdin said in surprise. 'Has something happened?'

His father smiled, although Aladdin could see that he was troubled. He didn't answer Aladdin's question; instead he said: 'Did you have a good day at school? I haven't seen you since you got home.' As if it was Aladdin and not him who had been busy all afternoon and evening.

'We were working on our projects. I wrote about the missing silver,' he said.

His father nodded as if he was thinking about what Aladdin had just told him. 'That sounds nice,' he said eventually. His voice sounded really weird.

'Has something happened?' Aladdin asked again, sitting down on the bed.

His father stroked his chin, which was not a good sign. He usually did that when he was worried about something.

'Yes,' he said with a heavy sigh. 'I'm afraid it has. Your grandfather has been taken ill, and I have to go to Turkey. Tonight. I'm flying from Copenhagen at midnight.'

Aladdin went cold all over. He loved his grandfather.

'How bad is he?'

His father looked upset. 'I'm afraid it's serious.'

'But he's not even old!'

His father had to smile. 'Your grandfather will be eighty-one in a few weeks. That's quite old, especially as he's had such a hard life.'

Aladdin knew that, of course, but he still felt sad. And angry, although he didn't know who he was angry with.

'When will you be back?' he asked.

'Next week, I hope. I've found someone to help your mum in the restaurant while I'm away.'

'I want to come with you,' Aladdin said.

'That's out of the question,' his father said. 'You have to go to school.'

'But if Grandpa dies—' Aladdin broke off; there was a huge lump in his throat.

'If Grandpa gets worse and I think he's going to die, then I promise to send for you,' his father said, stroking Aladdin's back.

'If Grandma ends up on her own, she'll have to come and live with us,' Aladdin said.

He felt his father stiffen.

'Grandma loves Turkey far too much to think of moving here,' he said. 'And besides, the rest of our family is there, not here. But it was a kind thought.'

There, not here. Such a huge difference.

His father cleared his throat. 'There was something else I wanted to talk to you about.'

Aladdin curled up inside; he knew what was coming.

'It's something your mum and I have been discussing for a while,' his father began. 'To tell the truth, things aren't going too well for us these days.'

It was as if Aladdin's ears were no longer working. He couldn't hear a word his father was saying. There was a book on the floor. Aladdin couldn't take his eyes off it. His father's voice kept on talking, but Aladdin just kept on staring at the book. He didn't want to hear what his father was saying, and he didn't want to let on that he'd been eavesdropping.

In the end he couldn't stand it any longer. His father was going on and on.

'So the thing is, Mum and I have been wondering if it might be better to move back to Turkey,' he said. 'We could give it a try, see how we feel. I mean, Sweden will still be here if we change our minds.'

When Aladdin didn't say anything, his father went on: 'We wouldn't go back to Ankara; we'd try one of the holiday resorts by the sea. You know how much the Swedes love their holidays in Turkey. There are real opportunities for us to open both a restaurant and a hotel there. It would be . . . an adventure. For the whole family.'

At last Aladdin managed to drag his gaze away from the book on the floor. 'I don't want an adventure,' he said. 'I want to stay here.'

Now it was his father's turn to look away. 'I can understand that,' he said quietly. 'But we need to be able to live a good life, Aladdin. All three of us. And here in Sweden . . .' He made a weary gesture with his hand. 'Things are changing. Åhus and the people who live here are changing. Look at all the fuss about the refugee boat, for example.'

Aladdin's eyes widened. 'But the refugee boat has nothing to do with us!'

'That's true in a way,' his father said. 'But a lot of people who live here are very angry, and think the people on the boat should go back where they came from, while others, like us, are putting out food for them.'

Aladdin sat up straight. 'But in that case we definitely have to stay here,' he said angrily. 'What if everyone who's prepared to share just packs up and leaves?'

His father laughed. 'We'll talk about this when I get back. I have to go and pack.'

He got up and left Aladdin alone in his room.

I'm never going to leave here, Aladdin thought. *Never!*

And he made himself a promise. He would fight with every ounce of his strength to stay in Åhus.

Chapter Twenty

The water tower felt empty without Dad. Aladdin's mother and a family friend were running the restaurant, while Aladdin went off to school as usual. He couldn't wait for the afternoon and the meeting with Ella. Time was running short. They had to find the silver, whatever it took. If they weren't allowed to keep it, perhaps there would be a reward. The papers were bound to write about it too, which meant that more people would want to eat at the Turk in the Tower. More customers, more money.

The kitchen was filled with the aroma of cinnamon when Aladdin got home from school. His mother was stirring a big bowl of mince, looking a bit stressed, and Mats was washing up.

'Has Dad called?' Aladdin asked.

'Yes, the journey went well. He sends his love.'

'How's Grandpa?'

'Not too good, but not quite as bad as Grandma said.'

Aladdin didn't really know what that meant. So Grandpa was ill, but not seriously ill?

He went and stood beside his mother. 'Did Dad say anything else about moving to Turkey?'

His mother looked away. 'No. Listen, sweetheart, I really haven't got time to talk about this right now.'

She picked up the bowl of mince and went over to the cooker. Aladdin didn't say anything. If they moved to Turkey, perhaps Mum and Dad would be able to work less. On days like this, he wished his parents had ordinary jobs.

'Me and Billie are going to meet a lady who might know something about the missing silver,' he said. 'I'll be back for supper.'

'That's nice,' his mother said.

'Mmm. If we find the silver, we might get a reward.'

'Lovely.'

He looked at his mother, who was standing with her back to him. Lovely? Was she even listening to what he said?

'I've bought a miniature pig,' Aladdin said.

His mother didn't react. 'That sounds great,' she said. 'Shall we have a chat about it tomorrow?'

Aladdin didn't answer; he left the kitchen and went down to his room. He really didn't want a miniature pig, he just wanted everything to get back to normal.

Köpmannagatan was almost deserted when Billie and Aladdin made their way to the café. Sometimes Aladdin thought it would be nice if Åhus was bigger, so that all the shops weren't on just one street.

He and Billie slithered along in the snow. It was a long time since they had seen Ella. Aladdin remembered only too well how they had felt when they cycled to her house through the pouring rain. Her cats had been afraid of the thunderstorm, and had hidden underneath the table. The whole thing had been very stressful.

When they reached the middle of Köpmannagatan, they suddenly heard sirens, and two police cars shot past them at full speed.

'I wonder where they're going,' Billie said, gazing after the cars.

A man standing nearby heard her. 'I think there's a fire on board the refugee boat,' he said.

Aladdin and Billie stopped dead.

'So where are the fire engines?' Aladdin wondered.

A second later they heard and saw the big red vehicles approaching. Aladdin covered his ears.

'That's terrible,' Billie said as the fire engines disappeared in the direction of the harbour.

Aladdin was more curious than frightened. 'Come on, let's get down there!' he shouted, breaking into a run.

'We haven't got time!' Billie called out behind him.

'Yes we have, if we get a move on!'

It didn't take many minutes to run down to the harbour and the refugee boat.

The man on the pavement had been right. There was smoke rising from the boat, but they couldn't see any flames. A few people were hanging around on the quayside to see what was going on.

'What's happened?' Aladdin asked a girl.

'Apparently some kind of heater went wrong and caught fire. I don't think it's serious; no one on board is hurt.'

A small group of people were huddled together a little further down the quayside; he assumed they were the refugees. They all looked upset as they stood there staring at the smoke. Where would they go if they couldn't stay on the boat?

Aladdin noticed that some of them were children. He quickly checked to see if any were wearing short trousers, but they weren't.

'Let's go,' Billie said, tugging at his arm.

They headed back to Köpmannagatan. The snow made all the houses and buildings look the same. Aladdin wondered what it was like if you'd never seen snow.

The Kringlan café was busy. They were fifteen minutes late by the time they arrived.

'I hope she's still here,' Aladdin said.

Ella was important. Without her they wouldn't be able to find the silver, Aladdin was sure of it.

Chapter Twenty-One

Ella was indeed still there, waiting patiently at a corner table. When she caught sight of them, she broke into a smile.

'How lovely to see you both again,' she said.

Aladdin and Billie greeted her politely and each pulled out a chair to sit down.

'Mind you don't sit on Erland, my dear,' Ella said to Aladdin.

He looked down at the chair and realized there was a cat carrier on it. Erland must be the cat.

'Sorry!' he said. 'I didn't see him.'

'He's my latest cat,' Ella explained. 'You could say he's a little baby. That's why I brought him along; he doesn't like being on his own.'

'He's gorgeous,' Billie said, peering into the carrier.

'You're covered in snow,' Ella said, nodding at their jackets. How about a hot chocolate?'

Ella went over to the counter, and Billie leaned over to Aladdin.

'We need to ask her about the Silver Boy,' she said. 'Even though the priest told us not to take any notice of what she said.'

'Of course,' Aladdin agreed. 'I hope she's brought lots of photographs to show us.'

Full of anticipation, he looked at the large hand-bag Ella had left on her chair. To be honest, he had no idea what he was hoping to learn from Ella. If only she could give them a clue about the missing silver and who had taken it.

Ella returned with two cups of steaming hot chocolate. 'You two really know how to pick a house,' she laughed. 'First of all Billie moved into the haunted house on Sparrisvägen, and now Aladdin's moved into the silversmith's house. Marvellous!'

'I don't live in a haunted house,' Billie said.

'No? So the ceiling light in the living room has stopped swinging to and fro?'

Billie didn't answer; she took a sip of her hot chocolate instead.

'What do you mean, I've moved into the silversmith's house?' Aladdin said. 'The water tower was built after the workshop was destroyed.'

Ella stirred her coffee. 'I don't think that will matter to the Silver Boy,' she said. 'The water tower is exactly where the workshop used to be, so that's where he'll be looking.'

'The Silver Boy,' Aladdin said as the colour drained from his face.

'Exactly.' Ella lowered her voice. 'The Silver Boy. He's about your age. It wouldn't surprise me if he tries to contact you, because he needs your help.'

'With what?'

'He needs you to help him find the missing silver, of course.'

This was a good start. They had only just sat down, and already Ella had mentioned both the Silver Boy and the silver.

There was a rustling sound from the cat carrier as Erland stretched.

'I don't understand who the Silver Boy is,' Aladdin said slowly.

'He's Orvar's son.'

Aladdin burned his mouth on the hot chocolate and put down his cup. 'Orvar's son? But I thought he died in an accident,' he said, thoroughly confused.

'Indeed he did,' Ella said. 'Indeed he did.'

She leaned across the table. With her dark eyes and grey hair she reminded Aladdin of his grandmother. She drew her green shawl more tightly around her shoulders.

'He died, but they say he stayed here in Åhus as a ghost – to keep his father company when his wife went off and left him. And to help his father.'

Aladdin reminded himself that he didn't believe in ghosts. Not really. But there was something spellbinding about Ella's story. Something that made him listen very carefully.

'Help him with what?' Billie wanted to know.

'To find the missing silver.'

'Why did he want to do that?' Aladdin asked.

'Does, not did,' Ella corrected him. 'The silver has never been found, and the Silver Boy is still searching. So that he can put things right.'

Billie shuffled uncomfortably. 'How do you know all this? How do you know that the Silver Boy exists, and that he's looking for the silver?'

'For the same reason as I knew quite a bit about what had happened in your house,' Ella said. 'I've lived here for a long time. I know people. People who have seen and heard things. Several of them have seen the Silver Boy, particularly at this time of year.'

Aladdin sighed. 'But if it wasn't Orvar who took the silver, then who was it?'

'That I don't know,' Ella admitted. 'It wasn't necessarily someone who disliked the silversmith; thieves are thieves, and they just steal things. Or it could have been the silversmith himself.'

Aladdin looked up. 'Do you believe that? Could it have been the silversmith?'

Ella shrugged. 'Who knows? It was the perfect way to ruin Orvar's life. The whole thing could have been an act of revenge.'

This wasn't what Aladdin had been hoping to hear. They had to find out for sure who the thief was, otherwise the silver would never be found.

Finding out that the Silver Boy had been searching for a hundred years without success wasn't exactly encouraging, to say the least. How on earth were Aladdin and Billie going to be able to find it in just a few weeks?

Chapter Twenty-Two

'I can see you're disappointed,' Ella said. 'Perhaps you'd like to look at some photographs instead?'

She opened her handbag and took out a cardboard box. 'I picked this up from the church archive on my way here. I hope I've brought everything.'

She opened the lid and peered into the box. 'Let's see,' she said. 'Here's an old picture of the silversmith's workshop.' She handed Aladdin a black-and-white photograph.

'It's so small!' Billie said.

'There are bigger ones too,' Ella said, passing them another picture.

This time they could see the silversmith more clearly. He was looking straight into the camera, a serious expression on his face.

'That was taken three months before the workshop was destroyed,' Ella said. 'The church had just placed the order for new silverware, and took the opportunity to photograph the silversmith.'

Aladdin thought he looked old. It was the same when he looked at black-and-white photographs of his grandparents; they looked old, even when they were young.

'And this is Orvar. This picture was taken at his son's funeral. The woman next to Orvar is his wife – she left him, as you know. On the right is their dog, and this is their younger son.'

It was a terrible image. The woman looked as if she had been crying for weeks on end; even the dog looked sad. You couldn't see the man properly; he was turning away from the camera.

'Nice dog,' Billie said.

Aladdin thought so too. 'He's wearing a very fancy collar,' he said, pointing.

'That dog became Orvar's closest friend,' Ella sighed. 'He had no one else after his wife left. This is a close-up of him – the dog, I mean.'

'Why does the church have an old picture of a dog?' Billie wanted to know.

'Orvar used to lend him to the priest and his family as a guard dog from time to time. The children loved him.'

The photograph showed only the dog's head and his collar; this time he looked really happy.

'I also managed to dig out a picture of the woman both Orvar and the silversmith wanted to marry,' Ella said, producing yet another picture from the box.

Aladdin could well understand why Orvar and the silversmith had clashed over this girl. She was very pretty – a bit like Billie, in fact.

'Nice dress,' Billie said.

'Don't you have any more pictures of Orvar?' Aladdin asked. 'I couldn't really see what he looked like in the other one.'

'I'm sure I have . . . Let's see . . .'

They were happy to wait; the café was warm and cosy. Aladdin started to wonder where he would hide a pile of stolen silver. He would probably bury it somewhere. Or sell it. After all, that was why people stole stuff, wasn't it? To make money.

Aladdin felt his heart sink. They would never find the silver.

'Here we are,' Ella said. 'This is Orvar. I wanted to find a picture with his son – the Silver Boy – but there doesn't seem to be one.' She passed the photograph across.

Billie and Aladdin stared at it. Neither of them said a word. Aladdin's heart was pounding so hard he thought it must be showing through his jumper.

'It can't be true,' Billie whispered.

'What?' Ella demanded. 'What can't be true?'

But she didn't get an answer. Aladdin couldn't take his eyes off the photograph. This time Orvar was staring straight into the camera. And he looked exactly like someone Aladdin knew very well.

Orvar was the spitting image of Mats.

It was Billie who eventually explained to Ella why they were so excited; Aladdin was so stunned that he couldn't say a word.

'So there's a man working in your restaurant who looks exactly like Orvar?' Ella said slowly.

'Yes,' Aladdin managed eventually.

He felt as if they had found out something really important; something that could explain how everything hung together – but right now he didn't understand it.

'In that case, Mats must be Orvar's great-grandson. I'd heard there was still a relative of Orvar's living in Åhus, but I had no idea who it was,' Ella said.

Aladdin was trying to work out how Mats could be related to Orvar.

'Think about it,' Ella said. 'Orvar had two sons. One of them died – the Silver Boy. The other moved to Kristianstad with his mother. So that boy must be Mats's grandfather.'

Aladdin counted backwards in his head. Yes, that would work.

'Perhaps it's just a coincidence that they're so alike,' he said when he had calmed down a bit. He stared at the photograph again.

'I don't think so,' Billie said. 'They could be the same person.'

'We have to talk to Mats,' Aladdin decided.

'What for?' Billie said. 'What are you going to say?'

'I've no idea. He might know something. About Orvar. If they were related.'

Ella sighed. 'I wouldn't get your hopes up too much. If he's like his great-grandfather, he won't be much of a one for talking. Orvar was well known around here for being a miserable soul.'

Aladdin nodded. Mats had the same reputation.

'Can we borrow this photograph?' he said. 'I'd like to have it with me when I speak to Mats.'

He thought about the dream he'd had on the night they slept in the restaurant – about the boy in the short trousers who had come to ask for his help in finding the silver.

Talk to Ella, the boy had said.

And now they were sitting here doing exactly that. Talking to Ella. Aladdin didn't understand how he could have dreamed something so strange that had actually come true.

'Of course you can,' Ella replied. 'Give it back to the priest when you've finished with it.'

Aladdin tucked it away carefully in his pocket.

'Are you sure you haven't got a picture of the Silver Boy?'

Ella shook her head sadly. 'I'm sorry, I haven't. Why do you ask? Do you think you've seen him?' She sounded curious.

Aladdin shuffled on his chair. 'Of course not,' he said. 'I don't believe in ghosts.'

But he couldn't help wondering. The boy in the short trousers, who came and went as he wished. Without leaving any footprints in the snow. Could he be—?

Ella laughed delightedly. 'So you say! I can see you've got something on your mind!'

Aladdin swallowed hard and refused to meet her gaze.

If it hadn't been for that stupid dream, Aladdin would never have started to wonder. But he had to ask himself:

Could the boy in the short trousers be the Silver Boy?

Chapter Twenty-Three

A little while later, Billie and Aladdin were standing outside the café. Ella had promised to leave the box of photographs with the priest, just in case they needed it again.

Aladdin breathed in the cold air. It was already dark.

'Do you think we'll ever find the silver?' Billie asked. She looked downhearted.

'I think we will,' Aladdin said quietly. 'If we really try.'

'But what about the Silver Boy?' Billie sounded dubious. 'Do you believe all that as well?'

Aladdin didn't know what to think. 'The Silver Boy is kind of irrelevant,' he said. 'It's the silver that's important.'

Billie nodded slowly.

'I think we ought to speak to Mats,' Aladdin said.

'About the silver?'

'About Orvar. If we feel brave enough, we could ask about the children in his cellar too.'

Billie didn't look too sure about that. 'I don't really—' she began.

'Or,' Aladdin broke in, 'we just go round to his house again, check if we can see the children. I know he's at work right now.'

Billie still didn't seem convinced, but Aladdin was determined.

'There's something weird about all this,' he said. 'Don't you think it's strange that Mats looks just like Orvar? And I want to know why there are two kids in his cellar.'

He set off along the street. 'Come with me if you want,' he said over his shoulder. 'Otherwise I'll go on my own.'

Billie sighed. 'OK, I'll come. But first we need to go to the bus stop.'

Aladdin stopped. 'Why?'

'Because I promised to meet Simona. She'll be here in fifteen minutes.'

*

The bus was early, so Simona was already waiting in the shelter. She couldn't believe her ears when they told her what they were planning to do.

'Are you crazy?' she said. 'You want to go back to Mats's house?'

She calmed down when Aladdin assured her that Mats would be at work for the next few hours. It was snowing again as they walked quickly away from the bus stop; big flakes that were almost like miniature snowballs drifted down onto their heads and shoulders. Aladdin couldn't have cared less. He was bursting with energy.

The snow formed little clouds around their feet as they half ran along the street. Once again Aladdin thought about the boy in the short trousers who had walked through the snow without leaving a single footprint.

I must have imagined it, he told himself for the hundredth time. *I was mistaken. The Silver Boy doesn't exist. He isn't real.*

Mats's house looked deserted; there were no lights showing through the large windows facing the street.

'It looks as if he's moved out,' Simona said. The others agreed. They hesitated on the drive; what should they do now? Should all three of them simply go charging in? What would they say if Mats came home, against all expectation?

'We do a runner,' Aladdin decided.

'Again?' Simona said.

'Again.'

As if on a given signal, the three of them walked towards the house.

'Where are we going?' Billie asked. 'Round the back, where Simona saw the children through the cellar window?'

'Let's start at the front,' Aladdin suggested.

They hadn't discussed it, but they stuck together. None of them wanted to be on their own. They moved towards the windows next to the front door; Aladdin had to stand on tiptoe in order to be able to see inside.

'Why don't we try the door?' Simona said. 'He might have forgotten to lock up.'

'No chance,' Billie said immediately.

'Isn't that illegal?' Aladdin said tentatively. 'Going into someone else's house?'

'What's that got to do with anything?' Simona said. 'What if those children are locked in the cellar? We have to let them out!'

But the very idea of sneaking into Mats's house made Aladdin go cold all over, so they settled for looking through the windows instead.

They couldn't see anything out of the ordinary. In the living room there were two sofas that Aladdin thought were particularly ugly, but Mats probably didn't share his opinion. There was a table covered in papers and magazines, and the biggest TV Aladdin had ever seen.

'He must love watching films,' Simona said. 'Or football.'

They moved on. Through the next window they saw what seemed to be a bedroom, and through the next an office.

In spite of the fact that Aladdin was sure Mats wouldn't be coming home, he felt nervous. His mother would go mad if she found out they were creeping around Mats's garden and peering through his windows.

'This is a waste of time,' Simona said.

They crouched down and looked through the cellar windows, one by one.

'I saw the children through the last window,' Simona said quietly, as if she was afraid that someone might hear.

Aladdin didn't know why he thought the children were important; perhaps it was because the way Simona had described them made him think of the boy in the short trousers. But most of all he wanted to know why Mats had two children in his cellar.

Eventually they reached the right window. Aladdin was so tense that he held his breath as he peeped in.

'I can't see a thing,' Billie whispered. 'It's too dark.'

Aladdin pressed his nose against the cold glass, but it was no good. He was just about to step back when something flashed inside.

'Did you see that?' he whispered. The girls nodded. They moved back so that they would be less visible; perhaps someone was sitting there in the darkness, staring out.

Aladdin had to take another look.

This time he could see a faint glow from one corner of the room. It was difficult to make out, but it seemed as if someone was holding a torch. The beam illuminated a number of items lying on the floor.

A big ball.

A skipping rope.

An old teddy bear.

Aladdin's heart was pounding so hard it was threatening to burst out of his chest. The person holding the torch slowly got to his or her feet and moved towards the centre of the room.

It was a child.

A boy.

A boy in short trousers and a thick woolly jumper.

The boy glanced up at the window; Aladdin, Billie and Simona threw themselves backwards into the snow, afraid of being spotted.

'Is that the same boy who's been creeping around your place?' Billie asked breathlessly.

'I don't know,' Aladdin said. 'I only saw him for a second.'

He edged back to the window and peeped in again.

Could this be the boy he had seen so many times? He still wasn't sure. They were very similar, but . . . No, he couldn't be certain. He backed away from the window.

'I didn't see the girl this time,' Simona said. 'There was a girl there before.'

Aladdin looked around. It was snowing heavily now. He must hurry home for tea.

'Could Mats have given the restaurant key to one of the children?' Billie wondered as they left the garden.

'So they could go in and help themselves to food, you mean?'

'Yes.'

'Maybe.'

Aladdin suddenly felt confused. He had thought it was the boy in the short trousers who was taking the food, but if that was the same boy he had just seen in the cellar, could he still be the thief?

'You ought to check tonight,' Simona said. 'Wait for a little while after you've put out the bag of food; if you hide by the window, you ought to be able to see who comes and picks it up.'

Aladdin thought that was a good idea. It would be useful to know who was collecting the food; he had a feeling that everything hung together somehow.

The stolen food.

The children in the cellar.

The boy in the short trousers.

And how did the missing silver fit in?

'I think the children in the cellar are from the refugee boat,' Billie said.

Aladdin thought so too. But what were they doing with Mats?

As they walked along the street, Aladdin glanced back over his shoulder. He stopped dead.

The snow had almost covered their footprints.

That must be what happened outside the church, he thought. *The snow covered the boy's footprints, and it happened so quickly that I didn't realize.*

He set off again. It was a good job it was snowing so heavily; if Mats looked around the garden when he got home, there would be no sign that they had ever been there.

Chapter Twenty-Four

There was a lot to do in the restaurant that evening. After he had eaten, Aladdin sat down at his desk. He had homework to do, but he was itching with impatience. He wished everyone would go home so that they could close up and leave the food out on the steps. Then at last he would find out who came to pick it up.

His mobile phone rang; he felt a warm glow when he saw who it was.

'Hi there!' his dad said. 'How are you and Mum getting on?'

Aladdin guessed that it must be expensive to call from Turkey, so he quickly started chatting about all kinds of things – about the missing silver, and about their second visit to the church. But he didn't mention Ella, or the photograph of the man who looked exactly like Mats.

'What will you do if you find the silver?' his father asked.

'Try to sell it,' Aladdin said quickly. 'So that we can stay in Åhus.'

His father didn't say anything.

Aladdin's mouth went dry. 'Unless the church wants it, of course,' he said in a thin voice. 'I mean, they'd already paid for it when it disappeared.'

Still his father didn't speak.

Aladdin cleared his throat. 'But I'm sure I'll get a reward,' he went on. 'And it will be in the papers, so more people will hear about the restaurant.'

'That all sounds marvellous,' his father said. 'But . . .'

The line crackled, and Aladdin pressed the phone closer to his ear.

'I can't hear you,' he said.

His father's voice sounded so distant, so shaky. 'I said we can talk about that when I get home. I've already had some new ideas down here. We could have a fantastic life on the coast, Aladdin. Think what fun you'd have if Billie and Simona came to visit!'

Aladdin could feel his throat closing up. It sounded as if the decision had already been made. 'But we have a good life here,' he said, trying to sound firm.

'Indeed we do,' his father agreed. 'But not as good as it used to be. Listen, I have to go. Grandpa sends his love; he's feeling much better. Give Mum a hug from me.' And then he was gone.

Aladdin put down the phone, trying not to cry. He wasn't very successful; a few stubborn tears escaped, trickling down his cheek and dripping off his chin. Billie had thought her mum was being unfair when she insisted they move twelve miles from Kristianstad to Åhus; Aladdin's father wanted him to move all the way to Turkey.

Why did everything have to be so complicated, particularly right now? Aladdin glanced at his books; his homework would have to wait until tomorrow. He was too angry and upset to tackle it now.

For a while he wondered whether to go up to the restaurant to talk to his mother, explain that he had no intention of moving. But she wouldn't have time to listen.

To his surprise, someone knocked on his bedroom door. He opened it to find Billie and Simona standing there, each with a rucksack.

'I told Mum we were staying over with you tonight,' Billie said. 'So you won't be on your own when you're waiting to see who picks up the bag of food. If that's OK with you, I mean . . .'

Aladdin was so pleased that he gave her a hug. He nodded. Of course it was OK.

'I'll just check with Mum,' he said, and ran up to the restaurant.

It was a very cold night. The snow glistened in the glow of the lights along the path leading to the tower. Aladdin's mother had no objections; Billie and Simona were welcome to stay over, even though it was the middle of the week. But they had to promise to get up early the next morning, in good time for school.

'How long are you going to carry on putting out food?' Mats muttered as Aladdin and his mother were packing a bag in the kitchen.

It was late, and the restaurant was about to close.

'As long as the refugee boat is in the harbour,' Aladdin's mother said.

'Right,' Mats said, turning away. 'How do you know it's someone from the boat who's taking the food?'

'We don't. But that's what we think. Aladdin has seen a boy in short trousers running around the area, and we believe he's from the boat.'

'Right,' Mats said again.

Why did he always have to be so grumpy? Aladdin picked up the bag and hurried down to Billie and Simona, who were waiting in his room.

Simona peered at the plastic boxes in the bag. 'What's in there?'

'Tonight it's meatballs, potatoes and bread.'

'Is it the same every night?' Billie asked.

'No, we try to give them a bit of variety.'

Earlier on they had eaten in front of the TV and played games; now they were just waiting for the restaurant to close so that they could put out the bag.

'By the way,' Simona said. 'I've had an idea. My dad is the boss of a big company here in Åhus. He's always saying that the food there is really terrible. What if they started ordering food from you? That would bring in lots of money!'

Aladdin's heart leaped with excitement. 'That would be brilliant,' he said.

'It's not definite,' Simona said, 'but I'll have a word with Dad.'

'Thank you!' Aladdin said.

He knew he had to find a way of helping his mum and dad if he wanted to stay in Åhus, otherwise he would be forced to move. Soon. Time was running out.

They heard footsteps on the stairs, followed by the sound of the front door closing and the key turning in the lock. Mum, of course; the last customers had gone home.

She called into Aladdin's room on her way back up. 'Everyone has gone, and we've finished clearing up,' she said. 'So I'm off to bed. Goodnight and sleep well, all of you.'

'Goodnight,' Aladdin said. 'I'll go and put the food out now.'

His mother went up to her room, and Aladdin ran downstairs with the carrier bag. The cold struck him as he opened the door. Billie and Simona waited just inside.

'What now?' Simona said. 'Are we going to hang around here all night?'

Standing in the hallway was nowhere near as comfortable as sitting in the restaurant, but in order to see who came for the food, they would have to peep out through the little window next to the door. Aladdin was ready; he had no intention of falling asleep this time!

'I don't think that's necessary,' he said. 'We can take it in turns to keep watch; I'll go first.'

'Yeah, right,' Billie said. 'You'll be asleep in two minutes!'

She and Simona started giggling.

'No I won't!' Aladdin protested.

'We'll see,' Simona said. 'Come and wake one of us up when you've had enough.'

'Or we'll come down and wake you up,' Billie said.

They shot up the stairs before Aladdin had a chance to answer. He was left alone in the hall-way. Hesitantly he reached out and switched off the light. It wasn't a good idea if it could be seen through the window; it might stop someone from picking up the bag of food.

Aladdin leaned against the wall and peered out. He didn't think he would have to wait too long. Nobody would want to hide out there when it was so cold.

That was just about the only advantage he could come up with when it came to moving to Turkey: it was warmer there. He tried to push away the thought of all his problems; perhaps Simona's father would be able to help them out.

Fingers crossed!

He couldn't hear a sound from anywhere in the tower. Mum must have gone to sleep right away, while Billie and Simona were probably whispering to one another, if they were still awake. They weren't particularly good at being quiet, but sometimes they managed it.

He wished the window was lower down; then at least he could have sat on the floor while he kept watch. He gazed out into the darkness. It was a good job the lights above the entrance to the restaurant were always left on, otherwise he wouldn't have been able to see a thing.

The minutes crawled by. Aladdin shuffled his feet. This wasn't anywhere near as creepy as staying up half the night in the restaurant. He kept on looking out, but there wasn't a soul in sight.

But at long last he thought he could see something. A man, casting a long shadow over the snow, was walking slowly towards the tower. Or was he on his way to somewhere else?

Aladdin swallowed hard. No, he was definitely heading for the tower.

So far Aladdin couldn't see his face, but even from a distance it was obvious that it wasn't the boy in the short trousers. He pressed himself against the wall, staring hard. If it wasn't the boy, then who was it?

He got his answer as the man walked up to the steps and bent down to pick up the bag.

It was Mats.

Chapter Twenty-Five

'Mats!' his mother said.

She was so surprised that she dropped her sandwich and looked up from the newspaper.

They had just sat down for breakfast – Aladdin, Billie, Simona and Aladdin's mother. They didn't usually have breakfast this early, but Billie and Simona had to catch the bus to Kristianstad in time for school.

Aladdin hadn't wanted to wake his mother in the middle of the night to tell her what he had seen, but he had to tell her now.

'It's true. I saw him with my own eyes. It's Mats who's been taking the food we leave out on the steps.'

His mother looked as if she was about to burst out laughing. 'So why did you spend half the night in the hallway peering out of the window, sweetheart? Couldn't you sleep?'

Billie and Simona snorted and took a bite of their sandwiches.

Aladdin's mother looked at them sharply. 'Are you two mixed up in this? Of course you are. I suppose that's why you stayed the night.'

She smiled and shook her head, but then her expression grew serious. 'Listen to me, all of you,' she said. 'I thought we talked about this back in the autumn, when you hid among the trees so that you could find out who was haunting Billie's house. I don't want you playing cops and robbers. You could get into serious trouble.'

Aladdin blushed. She was right, they had talked about it. He could still remember how he had felt, hiding among the pine trees and waiting to unmask the ghost.

'Mats didn't see me,' he said. 'And I was never going to open the door and go outside.'

'That doesn't matter,' his mother said. 'I still don't like it.'

She put down the paper and went to fetch some more coffee.

'What shall we do now?' Aladdin said.

'Do?'

'With Mats. Now that we know he's a thief.'

His mother frowned. 'We don't know any such thing,' she said.

'Yes you do!' Simona burst out, unable to keep quiet any longer.

Aladdin's mother slammed down the coffee pot. 'No we don't!' she snapped. 'All we know is that Mats took one bag of food from the steps. That doesn't necessarily mean anything. OK, so he knows we put out food, and that it's not meant for him; it's very bad to take food from someone who needs it more. But to go from that to the assumption that he's the one who's been stealing from the kitchen – no, I won't have it.'

Silence.

Aladdin stole a glance at Billie and Simona, hoping they wouldn't start talking about the time Simona had crept round the back of Mats's house to check if he was at home.

'And another thing,' his mother went on. 'If it was Mats who was stealing the food right from the start, then who's the boy in the short trousers?

Why was he hanging around here if not to steal food?'

'Maybe he knows Mats,' Aladdin suggested.

'Maybe he does. Anyway, I need to speak to Mats, but I have no intention of accusing him of stealing from the restaurant.'

Aladdin blinked. 'Are you crazy? You can't speak to Mats! You're not going to tell him I saw him, are you?'

'Calm down,' his mother said. 'I shall tell him I was in the hallway watching.'

She picked up her coffee cup and went towards the stairs. 'I need to go and get dressed. Clear the table when you've finished, please.'

At that point Aladdin remembered they had something else to talk about.

'Hang on,' he said. 'We've got something else to tell you – something good!'

His mother looked expectant; she liked surprises. Aladdin realized that it was a rare event these days.

'Simona's father might want to buy food from our restaurant for his company,' he said.

'Really?' His mother sounded quite taken aback.

'It's not definite, but I'm going to ask him,' Simona said.

'That's very sweet of you – thank you,' Aladdin's mother said. She didn't look particularly pleased; perhaps she thought nothing would come of it.

Aladdin felt a lump in his throat. If only Simona's father would help them! Otherwise he didn't know which way to turn.

At school they were given more time to work on their projects. Aladdin felt as if he had come to a dead end. He had worked much faster than his classmates, who seemed to think it was boring to write about people and places around Åhus. Aladdin didn't feel that way at all; this was the most enjoyable thing he had ever done in school. But now he felt as if he had more or less finished. He had read everything he could find, and he had spoken to the priest and to Ella. All that remained was to find the thief. And the silver.

The only person Aladdin hadn't spoken to yet was Mats. Who looked so much like Orvar. Who had two children in his cellar. And who evidently needed extra food. Aladdin had butterflies in his tummy. If only Mats wasn't so bad-tempered all the time!

He was almost sure that the boy in the short trousers was the boy he had seen in Mats's cellar. But not completely sure. There was a slim chance that the boy he had seen was in fact the Silver Boy. The fact that he didn't seem to have left any footprints in the snow had bothered Aladdin, but then he'd found an explanation for that the last time they were at Mats's house. It had been dark, and snowing heavily.

There are no ghosts, Aladdin thought for the hundredth time. *They definitely don't exist.*

He read through his notes once more, then he made a decision.

He would call Billie when he got home. They had to talk to Mats, preferably today. Aladdin had no intention of giving up before he found out who the children in the cellar were. He also wanted to know why Mats looked so much like Orvar.

Perhaps Mats held the final piece of the puzzle that would enable them to find the missing silver.

Chapter Twenty-Six

It was late afternoon by the time Billie arrived.

'Mum wasn't very happy when I said I was coming round here again,' she said. 'She thought I ought to stay in and do my homework, but I told her this was important.'

Aladdin was very grateful. He would have hated having to speak to Mats on his own. They would have to leave Simona out of things this time; she couldn't come down to Åhus at such short notice.

'By the way, Simona said to tell you she's had a chat with her dad, and he seemed to like the idea of your restaurant supplying food to his company. She'll give you a call as soon as she knows more.'

A ray of light. However, Aladdin couldn't allow himself to get too excited; nothing was decided yet. But he was keeping his fingers crossed!

They sat down on the stairs leading up to the restaurant and waited for Mats. According to the rota, he was supposed to finish at seven. Aladdin thought about the children in the cellar, and wondered what they did all day while Mats was at work. If they were living in his house, of course – but that was how it looked.

It wasn't the most comfortable place to sit and wait, but it was too cold to go outside. Customers passed them from time to time; they smiled at Billie and Aladdin, then hurried on. Mats should be here at any minute.

'Has your dad called again?' Billie asked.

'No. Well, he might have rung Mum, but I haven't spoken to him.'

They waited and waited. Billie shuffled impatiently. She wasn't allowed to stay out too late on school nights.

'He seems to be working overtime,' Aladdin said, glancing at his watch. It was almost seven fifteen.

'Shall we go up and get him?' Billie suggested. 'He might just be chatting to someone.'

Aladdin shook his head. It was better to stay where they were.

At last he came. Aladdin recognized the sound of Mats's footsteps immediately, and leaped to his feet. Game on!

A second later Mats appeared, tall and grim-faced. He looked as if talking to Billie and Aladdin was the last thing he wanted to do.

'Hi,' Aladdin said.

'Hi,' Mats grunted, pushing past them.

'Hang on! We want to talk to you!'

Mats stopped and turned round. 'What about?'

Aladdin couldn't get a single word out. Then he heard Billie say: 'We want to ask you about a relative of yours. Or someone we think is a relative of yours.'

'Someone who looks a lot like you,' Aladdin joined in.

Mats raised his eyebrows. 'And which relative might that be?' he said. He still sounded furious.

'Orvar,' Aladdin said. 'We'd like to talk to you about Orvar.'

There was a long silence. Two new customers came in and went up to the restaurant, edging their way past the little group on the stairs. Aladdin realized they would have to go somewhere else to talk; they couldn't stay here, blocking the way.

'Orvar?' Mats said. 'Which Orvar?'

Aladdin and Billie didn't say anything.

'The only Orvar I know of is my great-grandfather,' Mats said slowly. 'Is that who you mean?'

So it was true! Billie and Aladdin nodded.

'OK, so what do you want to know? Spit it out – I'm in a hurry. I have to get home.' Mats folded his arms.

'Perhaps we could go and sit down in the living room,' Aladdin suggested.

'No chance,' Mats snapped. 'We're fine here.'

Aladdin suppressed a sigh. 'We were just wondering whether you knew anything about the missing silver,' he said.

Mats's eyes widened slightly; Aladdin had obviously surprised him. 'Why would I?' he said angrily.

'Because you're related to Orvar,' Billie ventured.

'Orvar has been dead for a long time,' Mats said. 'I never even met him, for heaven's sake! How would I know anything about the silver?'

He paused and ran a hand wearily over his head; they could practically see the cogs turning in his brain.

'It all happened so many years ago,' he said eventually. 'Can't you just let it go? Leave the past where it is, dead and buried? It won't change anything if you find the silver, will it?'

Aladdin didn't agree.

Billie spoke up again. 'But Orvar is part of your family. Wouldn't it be good if the silver was found, so that everyone would know that he wasn't the thief?' Sometimes she could be a bit of a coward, but not this time.

Mats moved down a step. 'Like I said, I'm in a rush,' he said, reaching into his pocket. He pulled on a woolly hat and turned away. 'We can discuss this another day.'

But Aladdin had had enough. Yet another adult telling him they could 'discuss this another day'.

'Why are you in such a hurry?' he said. 'Is it because you know something about the silver that you don't want to tell us?'

When Mats didn't reply, Aladdin heard himself say: 'Or are you in a rush to get home to the children in your cellar?'

As soon as he'd spoken, he regretted it. Why had he said that? It almost sounded as if he thought Mats was keeping the children locked up.

But what was done was done.

Mats had gone bright red. He looked furious. 'What did you say?' he bellowed. 'I haven't got any children locked away!'

Aladdin and Billie tried to make themselves as small as possible.

'We saw them through your cellar window,' Aladdin whispered.

In fact he had seen only one of the children with his own eyes, but Simona had seen two.

Mats slowly shook his head. 'I knew this was going to cause problems,' he muttered. 'I just knew it.'

He sighed and leaned back against the wall. Then he straightened up, as if he had come up with an idea. 'Right, you're coming home with me,' he said firmly. 'Go and get your coats; my car's outside.'

Aladdin and Billie looked at one another. There was no way they were going anywhere with Mats, not when he was so angry.

At that moment Aladdin's mother appeared on the stairs. 'Goodness, are you still here, Mats?'

'I've just been having a chat with Billie and Aladdin,' he said. 'I'd like to take them back to my house for a while. If they want to come, of course, and if you don't mind. I've got some children staying with me, and I'd like Billie and Aladdin to meet them.'

'I don't mind at all,' Aladdin's mother said, 'but it's up to them whether or not they want to go. Who are these children?'

Mats managed a little smile. 'You could say they're the children of some good friends of mine.'

That swung it. It took less than two seconds for Billie and Aladdin to make up their minds. If Mats was prepared to speak so openly about the

children, then perhaps there was nothing dodgy
going on.

They were going to meet the children they
had seen in the cellar – and perhaps they would
find out more about Orvar and the silver at the
same time.

Chapter Twenty-Seven

Mats drove slowly through the village, past house after house with glowing windows. It was as dark as if it was the middle of the night. The light from the streetlamps seemed to bounce off the packed snow.

Aladdin and Billie sat in silence in the back seat. If only there had been another adult in the car. Mats was so bad-tempered. What if he was dangerous after all? What if he locked *them* up in the cellar?

How long will it be before Mum starts to wonder where we are? Aladdin thought to himself.

By the time they turned into the drive his pulse was racing, but he just couldn't keep quiet any longer.

'Who are they?' he said as he undid his seatbelt. 'The children – who are they?'

'You'll see,' Mats said tersely, getting out of the car.

Aladdin and Billie followed him to the front door; he unlocked it and let them in. He switched on the light in the hallway and kicked off his boots.

'Hello!' he shouted. 'I'm home!'

He walked through the house, switching on more lights as he went. There wasn't a sound; no one had answered his call. Billie and Aladdin were still standing in the hallway, not quite knowing what to do.

'Come on in,' Mats said. 'It usually takes a while before they come out.'

'Why?' Aladdin said. 'Are they hiding?'

Mats nodded. He looked sad. 'That's exactly what they're doing. They don't speak much Swedish. Or English. We usually communicate using a kind of sign language.'

The floor creaked as Aladdin and Billie followed Mats into the living room.

He waved a hand in the direction of the sofa. 'You're welcome to sit down,' he said. 'Can I get you anything? A glass of juice maybe?'

They both shook their heads. The sofa was soft as they sat down; the room smelled dusty, and as if it could do with some fresh air.

Aladdin looked at the huge TV he had seen through the window. 'Do you watch a lot of films?' he asked.

Mats brightened up a little. 'Yes – almost every night. I love films – the way you love your model planes, I guess.'

Aladdin had no idea that Mats knew he made model planes.

Mats sat down in an armchair opposite them. 'Right, I'd like to know why you've been creeping around here looking through my windows,' he said.

Aladdin shuffled uncomfortably. 'We wanted to know if you were the one stealing food from the restaurant,' he said eventually. 'Mum and Dad are having a few financial problems at the moment, and we wanted to track down the thief.'

'So it was your friend who was round the back of the house when I got back from the shops last week?' Mats said.

Billie and Aladdin both went bright red.

'Er, yes,' Aladdin stammered, then pulled himself together. 'But you'd lied to my dad. You said you were going to visit your mother, but that wasn't true. You were here all the time.'

'So you assumed I was the thief?'

'Yes,' Billie said, and Aladdin nodded in agreement.

Mats looked at them and laughed. 'Well, that wasn't such a bad guess,' he said wearily, 'because you were absolutely right. I did take all the food, but it wasn't for me. It was for the children. And for the others who are still on the refugee boat.'

Aladdin and Billie just stared at him.

So it had been Mats all along!

At that moment they heard footsteps on the stairs, and two children peeped in through the door: a girl wearing a skirt, and a boy in short trousers.

'Come on in,' Mats said, waving to them. 'Let's get this sorted out.'

Chapter Twenty-Eight

The children were called Nadia and Benjamin. They had travelled so far and for such a long time that Aladdin couldn't really keep up as Mats told their story. However, he understood that they had finally arrived in Åhus on the refugee boat. They had come all the way from Syria.

'I met Nadia and Benjamin's parents through a good friend. They asked if the children could stay with me while they tried to find a better solution, so that they can stay here in Sweden and live together.'

'You said they were hiding,' Aladdin said.

'That's what they do,' Mats explained. 'Their parents are seeking asylum in Sweden; they have a lot of enemies in their homeland. So many that their father is afraid that some might have followed them all the way to Sweden. Until he knows for sure, the children must be kept hidden. It's complicated, because they shouldn't really need to hide at all. Everything will be fine as long as they're allowed to stay in Åhus. Or somewhere else they can be safe.'

Mats sighed and scratched his head. 'I really hope they can stay, because otherwise I don't know what's going to happen to them.'

The children didn't seem to understand much of what was being said. They sat down on the floor, gazing up at Mats. Aladdin tried to understand what Mats was telling them: the children's parents had enemies in Syria, and therefore they must be allowed to stay in Sweden. And they were afraid that some of these enemies might have come here looking for them. Aladdin and his family had never had problems like that. Not as far as he knew, anyway.

It was annoying that Billie and Aladdin couldn't talk to the children; things would have been so much easier then. Easier and more fun. But if they stayed in Åhus, they might end up in the same school as Aladdin. He realized he was hoping that would happen; that Nadia and Benjamin would be his friends one day.

He couldn't take his eyes off Benjamin. He was so much like the boy in the short trousers!

'I see you're looking at Benjamin,' Mats said. 'Do you recognize him?'

'Maybe,' Aladdin mumbled.

'He's been hanging around the tower from time to time,' Mats said. 'He likes to wait for me to finish work. I've tried to explain that it's best if he doesn't leave the house, but of course he doesn't want to sit indoors hiding day after day.'

'Does he have any other clothes apart from the ones he's wearing now?' Aladdin asked tentatively.

'Of course!' Mats sounded cross again.

'It's just that I've seen a boy who looks like him,' Aladdin said hurriedly. 'I saw him in our cellar once; he was wearing a jacket and short trousers.'

Mats frowned. 'That might have been him ... I've tried to explain that it's too cold to go out in shorts, but he seems to wear thick socks, and his shorts do come down to his knees. But to be perfectly honest, I don't know what he puts on while I'm at work. Maybe he's just the kind of person who doesn't feel the cold.'

Once again Aladdin wished he could talk to the children; it would make everything so much simpler.

'So why did you take the food?' he asked instead. 'If you'd only asked, Mum and Dad would have given it to you.'

Mats pulled a face. 'I didn't really want to tell anyone about my house guests,' he said. 'That would have led to a whole lot of questions. Besides which, Nadia and Benjamin's parents said they couldn't stay with me if I told anyone about them.'

'But you said you gave some food to the people on the boat as well. Mum and Dad would have been happy to do that – after all, that's why we've been putting out a bag of supplies every night.'

Mats sighed. 'I know. I do know that. But I was so afraid that people would start gossiping about why I wanted to help the refugees. I made a huge mistake. And . . . I really didn't know your parents were having financial problems. I thought they had plenty of money, unlike me. I'll tell your mum everything. Tomorrow. I'd be grateful if you could keep this quiet until then; I'd rather she heard it from me.'

Aladdin nodded. 'But she already knows you took one of the bags of food.'

'She mentioned that today, but we didn't have time to talk about it,' Mats said. 'I promise I'll explain everything tomorrow.'

He looked at his watch. 'I need to make a start on dinner, so I'm afraid you'll have to go home.'

Aladdin was disappointed. They knew who the children were, and why the food had gone missing. But the silver . . . why was it so difficult to find out what had happened to it?

He couldn't help asking one more time. 'The missing silver . . . You don't know who took it?'

At first Mats looked so cross that Aladdin wished he hadn't said anything, but then his face cleared. He sat there for a long time, thinking about what to say.

'OK,' he said eventually, speaking so quietly that Billie and Aladdin had to lean forward to hear him. 'I've told you everything else, so you might as well hear this too.'

He scratched his beard and gazed into the distance. Aladdin and Billie waited, as taut as violin strings.

'I'm sure you know the story,' Mats went on, 'otherwise you wouldn't be here. You know that everyone thought it was Orvar, my great-grandfather, who took the silver in order to punish the silversmith, because he got the girl they were both in love with.'

Billie and Aladdin nodded eagerly.

'I don't really have much to add. This has been a source of great shame to my whole family, as you can imagine – the thought that one of our ancestors was a thief. I suppose that's why we've never said anything. But there's no getting away from it: Orvar really did take the silver.'

Both Billie and Aladdin gasped. For the first time they knew for sure: Orvar was the thief. Not the silversmith.

'Really?' Billie whispered.

'How do you know?' Aladdin asked. He was so excited that he could hardly sit still.

'When Orvar died, he left a will,' Mats explained. 'That's a kind of letter in which he wrote down what was to happen to his possessions after his death. In that same letter he admitted that he was the thief,

185

and said he had regretted his actions for over half his life.'

'So why didn't he just give back the silver?' Aladdin wondered.

'He couldn't. He was too ashamed. He said in his will that he hoped someone else would help him to return the silver, because he was too much of a coward.'

Aladdin's heart skipped a beat. 'Did he say where he'd hidden the silver?'

Mats sighed again. 'I'm afraid not. Hang on – I'll show you the will. I've got a copy in a file here somewhere.'

He left the room, and soon came back with a piece of paper that was so old it had gone yellow. It was a poor copy, but it was still possible to make out what it said.

As Aladdin and Billie pored over the document, he noticed that Benjamin and Nadia were watching them. He hoped he would be able to explain everything to them one day, when they'd been in Åhus long enough to learn Swedish.

The will was full of old-fashioned words; sometimes the expressions were so strange that it was hard to understand what they meant. But suddenly Aladdin came to a sentence that shocked him.

Orion is watching over the silver, it said.

'What does this mean?' he said to Mats, pointing to the words.

'Orion is a constellation, a group of stars,' Mats said. 'Our family assumed it meant he had left the silver lying out in the open, beneath the night sky, so that anyone could take it.'

Aladdin felt thoroughly deflated.

It was over.

Anyone could have taken the silver. Picked it up and kept quiet about it. They might even have moved away from the village. It was time to accept the inevitable: they were never going to find it. He couldn't remember when he had last felt so disappointed.

'I'm really sorry,' Mats said. 'I wish I had better news, but I haven't. And now it really is time for you to go home; I've got a thousand things to do.'

He took back the will and led the way to the front door.

Billie and Aladdin followed him; Billie gave the children a little wave as she left. They were sitting on the floor, talking quietly to one another. Nadia smiled and waved back. Aladdin looked at Benjamin.

'By the way, do you know who the Silver Boy is?' he said.

'That's just a ghost story; it's nonsense,' Mats said curtly.

'So you don't believe he's Orvar's son, still searching for the silver?'

'I don't believe in ghosts. On the other hand, I do believe in making up for things, in a way. Orvar did the wrong thing when he stole the silver, so the members of the family who are still around try to do some good. For example, that's why I'm helping Nadia and Benjamin. If everyone just made a bit more of an effort, a lot of things would be better,' he said.

It had started snowing again when Billie and Aladdin stepped outside.

Orion is watching over the silver.

Aladdin bit his lip. There was something about the name Orion that rang a bell, but he couldn't remember where he'd heard it before.

'I don't think we're going to find the silver,' Billie said.

'No, I don't think we are,' Aladdin agreed.

They walked through the falling snow in silence. Billie went home, and Aladdin carried on towards the tower. He couldn't stop thinking about Orion.

Where had he heard that name before?

Chapter Twenty-Nine

It was late when Aladdin's mother came in to say goodnight; she had been working hard.

'Don't read for too long, sweetheart,' she said.

But Aladdin wasn't reading; he was just lying there thinking, the thoughts whirling around in his head like birds. He thought about the children he had met but couldn't talk to. And he thought about Mats, trying to do some good because his great-grandfather had once done something very bad.

Aladdin didn't know why, but he had been kind of hoping that Orvar wasn't the thief, that it would turn out to be someone completely different. Most of all he had been hoping that they would find the silver. Quickly and easily. But it looked as if that wasn't going to happen. The silver was gone.

Orion is watching over the silver.

Aladdin tossed and turned. He knew he had heard or seen the name Orion before – but where?

Was it the priest who had mentioned Orion?

Or Ella, perhaps?

It was no good – however hard he tried, he just couldn't remember.

His thoughts turned to what his father had said on the phone: that they would talk when he came home. It sounded as if he had already made his decision, but he couldn't do that, could he? They were a family. That's what Mum and Dad always said: that everyone in the family counted.

Aladdin clenched his fists, seething with anger. If Mum and Dad moved to Turkey, they could go on their own. Aladdin had no intention of going with them.

The sound of the telephone woke him the next morning. He sat up in bed, still half asleep. Who was calling at this hour? It wasn't even seven o'clock!

He got out of bed and almost fell over a model plane on the floor. With clumsy fingers he picked up his phone from the desk.

'Hello?'

He heard Simona laughing.

'Hello yourself – have you just woken up?'

'No . . . yes . . . maybe.'

It was typical of Simona to ring this early, assuming that everyone else was up and about.

'I just spoke to Billie,' she said. 'She told me what happened yesterday.'

Billie? Was she awake at this time of the morning too? Standing there in his pyjamas, Aladdin could hardly remember a thing.

'It's a shame you still don't know where the silver is,' Simona went on.

'Yes,' Aladdin mumbled. 'It is.'

He went over to the window and pulled up the blind. It was still dark outside. Then he heard footsteps on the stairs: Mum, of course.

She tapped on his door. 'Aladdin?' she said quietly. 'Are you awake?'

'I'm on the phone,' he called out. 'I'll be up in a minute!'

He sat down at his desk. 'I haven't really got time to talk now,' he said to Simona. 'Did you want something in particular?'

'I just wanted to tell you that I spoke to Dad,' she replied. 'He's going to give your parents a call tomorrow. He's eaten at the Turk in the Tower several times, and he loves your food. So maybe things will turn out all right!'

Aladdin was so relieved that he almost let out a yell, but instead he just grinned. 'That's brilliant! I'll tell Mum.'

Now he didn't need the silver any more – this was much better!

'OK. And call me if you find out any more about the silver,' Simona said.

Aladdin promised. Then he dropped the phone and rushed upstairs to the kitchen, where his mum was busy laying the table for breakfast.

'That was Simona,' he said. 'Her dad's going to call you tomorrow.' Breathlessly he passed on what Simona had said.

When he had finished, his mother smiled and stroked his cheek. 'What wonderful friends you have,' she said.

But she didn't sound anywhere near as pleased as he had hoped. There was a photograph album lying on the kitchen table; Aladdin knew exactly which one it was. An album full of pictures of him as a little boy, when they had just arrived in Åhus.

'I was looking at it yesterday,' his mother said.

Aladdin had seen the photographs hundreds of times. His mother thought it was important to know your roots, as she put it. That meant knowing where you came from and how you became the person you were.

But that particular morning Aladdin had absolutely no desire to look at old photographs.

'Don't you think it's great that Simona's father is interested in our food?' he persisted. 'His company might place a really big order.'

His mother didn't say anything; she just stared at the album. Then she sat down opposite Aladdin.

'Of course,' she said. 'But . . . I spoke to your dad on the phone yesterday. We talked for ages. And I have to admit that I'm starting to like the idea of moving back to Turkey.'

Aladdin stared at her.

'I know it would be difficult for all three of us in some ways,' she went on. 'We haven't lived there for over ten years. But a little part of me has always longed to go back. And now it's such a popular holiday destination among the Swedes – people talk about Turkey all the time. We could have such a wonderful life down there on the coast. Just think – no more snow!' She laughed and pointed at the window. 'Just think,' she said again. 'No more horrible snow and cold! Doesn't that sound fantastic?'

At last Aladdin regained the ability to speak. 'No!' he shouted. 'No!'

Suddenly he was so angry that he shot out of his chair. All the anger and anxiety that had been building up suddenly exploded.

'No! There's no way I'm moving to Turkey! If you go, then you'll have to go without me! I'm staying right here in Åhus!'

Before his mother had a chance to speak, he rushed out and down to his room. He could hear the phone ringing upstairs; good – that meant she wouldn't come after him. He quickly pulled on his clothes and dashed into the bathroom to brush his teeth. Then he put on his jacket and shoes and raced off through the snow like a madman. All the way to Billie's house.

Panting and pouring with sweat, he hammered on the door. It was opened by Josef, Billie's mum's friend.

'Where's the fire?' he said. 'I thought you were going to break down the door!'

'Is Billie home?' Aladdin gasped.

Billie appeared next to Josef; her eyes widened when she saw the state Aladdin was in. 'Whatever's happened?' she said.

'Mum says we're moving,' Aladdin said. 'Can I come and live with you instead?'

Billie's mum invited Aladdin to stay for breakfast. They didn't have much time, she explained, because Billie had to catch the bus to Kristianstad.

'He can come and live with us, can't he?' Billie said.

Her mother glanced at Aladdin. 'Of course, but what do you think his parents are going to say?'

'I don't care,' Billie said crossly.

Billie's mum leaned across the kitchen table to Aladdin. 'Exactly what did your mum say?' she asked.

Aladdin put down his sandwich. He remembered practically word for word what his mother had said about the snow and the sunshine and how wonderful everything was going to be.

Billie's mum shook her head slowly. 'I think you're overreacting. It doesn't sound to me as if any decision has been made; I just think she's considering the idea. That's OK, isn't it?'

'No,' Aladdin said. 'They need to talk to me as well.'

'You're right, and that's exactly what they've done. This morning, for example.'

Josef sat down at the table with a cup of coffee in his hand. 'It must be difficult for your parents,' he said. 'I'm sure they only want what's best for you, but if they can't make the restaurant pay, what can they do? They have to try something else.'

'But why do they have to go all the way to Turkey?' Billie said crossly. 'Why can't they try something else here in Åhus?'

Her mother smiled. 'It's not quite that simple, sweetheart.'

'Yes it is.'

'No, Billie, I can assure you it isn't.'

Silence fell around the table.

'Billie told me about your quest to find the missing silver,' Josef said after a while.

Aladdin nodded.

'It's such a shame we didn't get anywhere,' Billie said.

'But you found a lead, didn't you?' her mother said.

Billie groaned. 'Yes, but it was no use. Something to do with Orion. Pointless.'

Once again Aladdin had the strange feeling that he had heard the name Orion in a different context. He took another bite of his sandwich. Finding the silver didn't seem so important any more.

'When I was little, I had a parrot called Orion,' Josef said with a laugh.

Billie rolled her eyes. 'You can't call a bird Orion!' she said.

There.

As soon as the words were out of Billie's mouth, Aladdin remembered where he had seen Orion.

'I know who Orion is!' he shouted. 'And I know where the silver is!'

Chapter Thirty

From Billie's house you could take a short cut to the village through the grove of tall pine trees on the other side of the road. Billie and Aladdin ran as fast as they could; neither of them said anything. The only sounds were the soughing of the wind in the treetops and the noise of the traffic beyond the grove.

'So where are we going?' Billie said when they slowed down to a walk because they couldn't run any more.

'To the church – I told you.'

'Yes, but why?'

Aladdin had no intention of telling her why – not until he was sure he had guessed correctly.

Billie's mum hadn't been very pleased when they ran off. Or to put it more accurately, she had been very cross.

'How urgent can it be?' she had said. 'You've both got to get to school!'

But right now neither Billie nor Aladdin could have cared less about school; this was more important.

'We need to have another look at those photographs,' Aladdin said. 'Ella said she would leave them with the priest.'

'What if he's not there?'

'He's bound to be,' Aladdin said, hoping he was right.

And he was, although he wasn't alone in the church. There were lots of other people there too. Elderly people. The priest seemed to be giving some kind of guided tour, talking about the pulpit and the organ in a loud voice.

Billie and Aladdin stopped dead in the doorway, completely taken aback. When they walked in, several people turned round. The priest smiled when he caught sight of them.

'More visitors who are up and about bright and early,' he said. 'Welcome – please take a seat. We won't be long.'

Neither Billie nor Aladdin were in the habit of going to church; nor were their parents. As Aladdin sat on the hard wooden pew waiting for the priest to finish his tour, he wondered why the church couldn't make things a bit more comfortable for visitors. For example, why not install rows of seats like the ones in cinemas? And why not sell popcorn and sweets to eat while the priest was talking?

Billie was sulking because Aladdin wouldn't tell her why they were there. He didn't care; he wasn't going to say a word until they'd seen the photographs. Then she would understand.

They waited quietly and patiently. In spite of the fact that it was boring and uncomfortable, Aladdin decided that he liked being in church. It was calming, somehow. Bearing in mind how angry he had been earlier on, it felt good to relax for a while.

I'm not moving, he thought to himself. *I'm just not. Not even for Grandma and Grandpa's sake.*

At last the guided tour was over.

'You're turning into the most regular church-goers in Åhus,' the priest said as he came over. 'How can I help you this time?'

Aladdin explained why they were there.

'So Ella said she was going to leave the photographs here?' the priest said, looking thoughtful. 'In that case we'd better go to my office and see if we can find them.'

The office was the smallest Aladdin had ever seen; there was barely room for all three of them.

'Let's see – where would she have put the pictures?' the priest said.

'There!' Billie immediately spotted the box Ella had brought to the café; it was on one of the bookshelves.

'You mean this?' the priest said, handing them the box.

Aladdin's hands were trembling as he lifted the lid.

'So show me,' Billie said impatiently.

Aladdin sorted carefully through the pictures, and at last he found what he was looking for: the close-up of Orvar's dog, the one the priest had taken because his children were so fond of it.

'Look,' he whispered, passing it to Billie.

She looked, but she still didn't get it.

He pointed. 'There. Look at the name tag on his collar.'

Aladdin heard Billie gasp.

Orion. That was what it said.

Without revealing where he had got the information, Aladdin told the priest where the silver was.

'But how do you know all this?'

'I promised not to tell,' Aladdin said.

'So Orvar was definitely the thief?' the priest said.

Aladdin shook his head. He had promised Mats that he would keep quiet about as much as possible, and he intended to keep that promise. 'I didn't say Orvar was the thief. I just said the silver is with the dog.'

He handed the photograph to the priest. If they could just find out where Orvar had buried his beloved dog, then they would also find the silver.

'How are we going to do that?' Billie asked.

'I can help you with that,' the priest said eagerly. 'If you wouldn't mind stepping out while I get changed, I'll show you Orion's grave.'

Aladdin and Billie went back into the church; apparently the priest didn't want to run around in his long robes searching for dead dogs. That was understandable, of course, but they were so impatient they could hardly sit still while they were waiting.

'Just imagine if we find the silver!' Billie said.

'Wouldn't that be amazing?' Aladdin agreed.

Billie looked at her watch. 'I'm going to be so late.'

'Me too, but at least I can say I was doing something connected to school.' Åsa would be seriously impressed if he finished off his project by revealing that the silver had been found.

'Simona's missing all this,' Billie said.

Aladdin grinned. 'She'll be furious.'

The priest appeared; he was almost unrecognizable. He was wearing a thick winter coat and a big fur hat, and he was carrying a spade.

'How are we going to be able to dig when it's so cold?' Aladdin wondered. 'Won't the ground be frozen?'

'You'll see,' the priest said.

He led the way out of the church and through the graveyard, with Aladdin following on behind, then Billie.

They were all so preoccupied that they didn't notice the boy in the short trousers peeping round the corner of the building. He watched them as they left the churchyard and carried on to the rectory.

'This is where my family and I live,' the priest explained. 'And this is where all my predecessors and their families have lived. When Orvar's dog died, the priest's children were terribly upset, so Orvar agreed to let them bury the dog in their garden. Here, to be precise.'

The priest stopped beneath a tree, where someone had stuck a little iron cross in the ground.

'No one ever considered moving the grave; it has been undisturbed all these years.'

The ground was completely covered in snow. Aladdin looked dubiously at the spade. How on earth were they going to be able to dig when everything was frozen solid?

He got his answer when the priest cleared away the snow to reveal a pile of stones.

'If I'm right, Orion is buried under stones, not soil,' he said.

He banged the pile of stones with his spade and loosened several of them. He stopped for a moment and looked at Billie and Aladdin, his expression serious.

'We'll move the stones and see what's underneath. If we don't find anything, then we'll try again in the spring, when the ground has softened. OK?'

They nodded nervously.

The priest chipped away at the pile, while Billie and Aladdin moved the stones to one side. At last there were just a few left. Carefully they lifted them off, then all three leaned forward and stared down at the ground.

There was nothing to see.

Aladdin felt a wave of disappointment. Had he expected the silver to be lying there waiting for him? No doubt one of Mats's relatives had read the will, realized who Orion was, and retrieved the silver.

The priest poked at the ground with his spade in various places; it was rock hard. Hopeless.

Except in one particular spot, where he managed to loosen a small clod of earth. Aladdin stiffened with excitement. Because there, sticking up out of the ground, was a scrap of material.

The priest straightened up. 'Look,' he said. 'An old sack.'

'Pull it out!' Aladdin said.

'I'll try. I'm just a bit worried in case . . .'

'In case what?' Billie said.

'In case the dog is in the sack.'

'We can just have a peep,' Aladdin said. 'And a feel. We don't need to drag the whole thing out.'

The priest agreed. Using the spade, he managed to expose a little more of the sack, then he crouched down and touched it. Slowly he turned and looked at Billie and Aladdin. 'I can hardly believe it,' he said, 'but I think we've found the missing silver.'

He ripped a hole in the fabric with his fingers. Aladdin and Billie crouched down on either side of him; then Aladdin fell on his knees in the snow, trying to see inside the sack.

'Wait,' the priest said.

He took a box of matches out of his pocket; there was a crackling sound as he struck one. He held the flame as close to the fabric as he could without setting it on fire.

'Now look,' he said to Aladdin.

Aladdin gazed into the sack.

He couldn't believe his eyes when he saw the glint of old, tarnished metal.

Chapter Thirty-One

They were in the priest's house, looking at the silver. He had spread newspaper all over the table, and placed the sack and the silver on top. You could hardly tell it was silver. All those years in the ground meant that it was damaged and dark in colour; Aladdin wondered what could be done with such old objects.

'I'll have to talk to the church council,' the priest explained. 'I know it was a long time ago, but the church did actually pay for most of these items. I don't know what will happen next, but of course you'll get a reward.'

A reward sounded good, but it was unlikely to be enough to persuade Aladdin's parents to stay in Åhus. Not if they'd already made up their minds.

Aladdin's elation and excitement gradually seeped away. When he got home, everything would be exactly the same as it had been this morning – miserable and awful.

The priest's wife brought them juice and biscuits, and they told her the story of how they had found the missing silver.

'And you're still not prepared to tell me who the thief was?' the priest said, glancing at the silver.

Aladdin shook his head.

'OK. By the way, don't forget to tell Ella what's happened.'

At last it was time to go home. The priest promised to call as soon as he knew what was to become of the silver.

Billie and Aladdin left the rectory garden in silence.

'Do you want me to come home with you?' Billie asked.

'No. Thanks for the offer, but it's OK.'

'Sure?'

'Absolutely.'

He must hurry home; his mum would be wondering where he was. Just like Åsa, his teacher.

'You know you can come and live with us if your parents decide to move,' Billie said seriously.

Aladdin nodded. The question was, would he want to do that? Or would he feel better living with Mum and Dad, wherever they were? He thought about the children in Mats's cellar. They hadn't seemed very happy to be there.

'I'll call you tonight,' he said.

Then he turned and set off towards the tower.

It was very quiet when he got home. Perhaps his mum had gone out. Quickly he went from room to room, and eventually he found her in the restaurant with a cup of coffee.

'Hi,' he said.

'Hi.'

He went over and pulled out a chair. 'Sorry I took off,' he said quietly.

His mother fingered her cup. 'I'm the one who should apologize,' she said. 'For not listening to you, and because your dad and I lied to you.'

She took a deep breath. Aladdin waited anxiously.

'I rang your dad,' she said slowly. 'We're not going to make any decision about moving until we've spoken to Simona's father. If he can help us, then we might be able to stay here. If not . . .' She paused. 'If not, then we'll have to look at other options, because we can't carry on like this. Your dad and I can't keep on working flat out; we never see you. Nor can we live with the constant worry that the money is going to run out. It was never like this in the past, and it's not going to be that way now. OK?'

Aladdin nodded. 'OK.'

His mother stroked his arm. 'So where have you been?'

His face brightened. 'To the priest's house,' he said.

'What on earth—?' his mother began.

'It's true! And guess what? We found it. We found the missing silver!'

His mother burst out laughing. She looked as if she might start crying. 'You're just like your dad,' she said. 'You think nothing is impossible.'

Aladdin blushed and shrugged.

Some things were difficult, and some things were easy.

But impossible . . . No, hardly anything was impossible.

Chapter Thirty-Two

It was December. Soon it would be Christmas. The snow melted, trickling along the streets. Aladdin finished his school project about the missing silver; his teacher led the applause when he stood up in front of the class and told everyone what had happened.

'What a story!' Åsa said.

Two weeks had passed since they dug up the sack in the rectory garden. The church had decided to keep the silver objects; Billie and Aladdin had received a generous reward, which they shared.

Aladdin still hadn't decided what to do with the money. Perhaps he would buy the biggest model plane he had ever owned.

His dad was back from Turkey. Simona's father had been in touch, and wanted to set up a catering contract between the Turk in the Tower and his company.

Aladdin's parents kept on talking about what they should do, over and over again. To begin with, Aladdin's father really wanted to move back to Turkey, but after a few days he seemed to remember how much he liked Åhus, and started to sound less sure of himself.

Eventually they decided to stay for a while longer.

'But there's one thing you have to understand, Aladdin,' his father said gravely. 'We can't live on fresh air. If the restaurant here in Åhus doesn't work, then we'll have to think of something else. We might have to move, and we should regard the fact that we could move back to Turkey as something positive. It's not everyone who has the choice of two countries.'

The people on the refugee boat had had to move. They couldn't stay there after the fire. According to the newspaper, they were living in apartments in Kristianstad on a temporary basis while they waited to hear whether they would be allowed to remain in Sweden. Once they had gone, the boat simply vanished. A man out walking his dog said he saw it sailing away in the middle of the night. Just like when it had first appeared in the harbour.

It wasn't only the refugee boat that vanished; the children who had been staying with Mats were gone too. They were living with their parents in Kristianstad. When Mats confessed everything, Aladdin's father wanted to sack him, but Aladdin spoke up for him. Mats hadn't stolen the food for himself, he had taken it to give to others.

'This isn't about who Mats gave the food to,' Aladdin's father said. 'It's about the fact that we can't trust him any more. He should have come to us and explained the situation, and we would have given him food. Perhaps not as much as he took, but whatever we could manage.'

'But he couldn't be sure of that,' Aladdin protested.

Eventually they decided that Mats could stay, but Aladdin noticed his father giving Mats a sidelong look from time to time.

'So we've found the silver, the refugee boat has gone, and the food thief has been caught,' Billie summarized. 'And best of all, you're staying in Åhus! Everything's back to normal.'

They were on their way to Ella's house to return the photographs they'd borrowed. They could have left them in the church, but Ella had been so kind that they wanted to go and see her.

They were also curious about what she thought the Silver Boy would do now that the silver had been found.

'I think he's at peace,' Ella said firmly.

They were standing in her hallway. Aladdin and Billie looked at one another.

'He won't be here in Åhus any more,' Ella said. 'Not now the silver has been returned to its rightful owner.'

'No,' Aladdin said; to tell the truth, he didn't really know what to say.

'Are you sure you never saw him?' Ella said, narrowing her eyes.

Aladdin nodded quickly. 'Of course not.'

'Wait here,' Ella said. She disappeared, and came back with a black-and-white photograph in her hand.

'I managed to find a picture of the Silver Boy – Orvar's son,' she said. 'It was in an old box I hadn't had time to go through.'

She handed the picture to Aladdin. 'Are you still sure you've never seen him?'

The boy in the photograph was wearing short trousers and a striped jumper. Aladdin swallowed hard, several times – because the boy bore a strong resemblance to the one he had seen in the garden and on the church steps. The boy who didn't leave any footprints in the snow.

If only he could be sure – really, really sure – that the snow had simply covered his tracks.

But I just don't know, he thought. *I don't know if it was Benjamin, who was staying with Mats. Or if it was the Silver Boy.*

Or both.

It occurred to him for the first time that it hadn't necessarily been the same boy each time, but he said to Ella: 'I'm sure. I've never seen him.'

She looked disappointed. 'Oh well, if you say so.'

As they were leaving, Billie looked at him.

'You're not sure at all, are you?'

'About what?'

'Whether the boy in the short trousers was one of the refugees, or whether he was the Silver Boy.'

Aladdin thought for a moment before he answered. 'I think it was the boy from the cellar that I saw. But no, I'm not absolutely certain.'

A large black bird flew past them and settled at the top of one of the pine trees.

'Me neither,' Billie admitted.

In silence they crossed the little footbridge over the river. Aladdin looked to the right and left, but there was no sign of the boy in the short trousers.

He decided it didn't matter any more. If the boy was from the refugee boat, he had somewhere to live now. And if it was the Silver Boy, then he had got what he wanted. Billie and Aladdin had found the silver. They hadn't said a word to anyone about Orvar's letter and his confession. Mats was right. Something that had happened a hundred years ago could remain in the past.

They headed towards the square and café Kringlan. It was just as Billie had said.

Everything was back to normal.

*

The boy in the short trousers followed them for one last time. Neither Billie nor Aladdin noticed him. Perhaps he was wondering whether to say something to them, but he didn't. Instead he turned off into the churchyard. He walked quickly, and disappeared round the side of the church.

But there was no sign of any footprints in the snow.